LOVE UNDER THE MISTLETOE

KRISTA LAKES

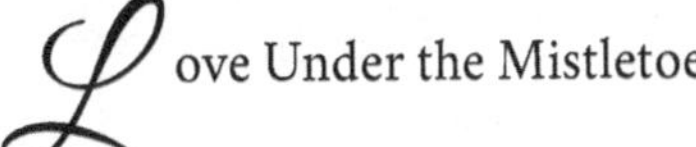
ove Under the Mistletoe

CAN a kiss under the mistletoe save Christmas?

Holly has always loved Christmas, but this year is different. As a school teacher, she's worried about her students, her dad, and her entire town. All of them are poised for a terrible Christmas, and there's nothing she can do about it.

The only bright spot in her life is the mysterious man she meets at the holiday party.

Nathan has always hated Christmas, but this year is different. As a billionaire, he's excited about his new plans for his company, but as always, it's all about the money. When he meets the bubbly woman who doesn't care about his wealth, love blossoms under the mistletoe.

It almost seems like magic.

But their lives are more intertwined than either of them originally thought. It turns out that Nathan's plan for the future of his company is the very thing that's destroying Holly's community.

Holly begins to understand why everyone refers to Nathan as a Scrooge, and she thinks that the wonderful man she shared a passionate weekend with was nothing more than a lie. Will Nathan be able to prove that she saw the real him?

Will Christmas magic prevail, or will their love vanish like a kiss under the mistletoe?

NYT Bestseller Krista Lakes brings you this brand new heartwarming holiday romance. This standalone novel will convince you that love can make the magic of Christmas real.

CHAPTER 1

*H*olly

HOLLY JONES PULLED out a red pen and started grading.

"Did you seriously bring your grading with you?" Aliyah asked, turning to look from the road to stare at her friend.

"Yes. And pay attention to the road, please," Holly replied, motioning to the twisting mountain road in front of them. "It's snowy and this pass is always slippery."

"Yes, Ms. Jones," Aliyah replied, sounding like one of their second-grade students. "You know this is supposed to be a vacation, right?"

"Yes." Holly circled and marked the writing assignment of her student in front of her. "But I'll only feel like I'm on vacation when these are done. I only have a couple left."

Aliyah shook her head sadly. "You work too hard."

"You work just as hard as I do," Holly replied. She slid a finished page back into her folder.

"I'm not the one grading papers right now," Aliyah said,

turning on the windshield wipers to brush away the big snowflakes. It was snowing harder the closer they got to the ski resort.

"That's because you're driving." Holly grinned at her. "So it's a good thing you're not grading papers."

"You are going to have fun this trip, right?"

"Yes. I promise to have fun," Holly replied, not looking up from her grading. She'd asked her students to write their three wishes for the holidays and wanted them ready to return to her students as soon as she got back from her trip.

"I'm serious. I don't know the last time you did something that wasn't work related."

"I do fun things," Holly insisted. "I did that 5k race in November. That was fun."

"That was a school fund-raiser and you ran one of the check-in desks." Aliyah gave Holly a disapproving glance. "Seriously, when's the last time you went out on a date? Or did something not sponsored by the PTA?"

Holly opened her mouth, but couldn't find an answer. "Uh..." She shrugged and tried to turn the question back onto Aliyah. "What do you do for fun? You're just as busy as I am."

"I went on a date with a fireman last week, remember? Captain McHotty?" Aliyah sighed with pleasure. "We played laser tag. We ate at a fancy restaurant that *didn't* have a teacher's discount."

Holly clicked her pen a couple of times. "Fine. Your point's made. I'm boring."

"You're not boring. You're stuck. You've focused only on work. You need a life outside of work."

"I know." Holly sighed. She wasn't sure how she'd become boring. She'd just become so focused on her students that she'd become blind to the world around her. Her dad often told her that she gave too much of herself, and she had a feeling she was doing it again. "But, at least it got us this weekend, right?"

"Partly," Aliyah acknowledged. "You've always been an amazing teacher. You earned this award. And you still deserve to have fun sometimes. It is possible to have both. You need some balance in your life."

The entire reason Aliyah and Holly were driving up to the mountains was for Holly to be awarded with the Educator's Award. She'd been nominated by her students and selected by a committee as the best teacher in the nation.

As such, she and a friend got to go stay at Blue Aspen Ski Resort for a weekend and go to a fancy party. The party was as much to honor her as to raise funds for education scholarships, so she was happy to be there and assist.

"I'm going to remember how to have fun this trip," Holly promised. "Just as soon as I finish these papers."

"Sure." Aliyah chuckled and rolled her eyes. "Will you hand me my sandwich?"

"Sandwich?" Holly frowned, looking around the interior of the car. "Where'd you get a sandwich?"

"At the gas station before we started up the pass," Aliyah replied. She pointed to the backseat. "It should be right back there."

Holly twisted around in her seat until she found a sandwich wrapped in plastic wrap. It had fallen off the seat and onto the floor. She held it up, making an unsure face.

"Are you sure you want to eat this?"

"It's wrapped in plastic. It's fine."

"It's not just that." Holly turned the sandwich around in her hands and grimaced. "It's a gas station sandwich."

"I'm hungry." Aliyah grabbed the sandwich from Holly's hands. She gave Holly a glare as she ripped open the plastic and took a big bite. "I've eaten worse at the school cafeteria."

"And that's why I bring my lunch," Holly murmured, shaking her head and going back to her grading.

"How's your dad?" Aliyah asked, her mouth full of sandwich. "Is he still closing the store?"

Holly paused her grading. "He's okay, and yeah. The store is still closing. He just can't make it work without Elements in town. They're his biggest customer. With them leaving, we just don't have the sales."

Aliyah shook her head. "Damn. I was hoping he was going to make it."

"Me too," Holly said. She looked down at her grading, but her eyes didn't want to focus on it. The biggest employer in town, Elements Computer Technologies, or ECT as everyone called it, had been bought by some big tech firm.

At first, the town thought it would be great. Paradigm was huge and had great growth potential. That was until Paradigm announced that they were moving ECT to San Francisco. Suddenly, a huge portion of the town was preparing to move across the country. Both parts of the population, those moving and those staying, were in a panic.

Holly tried not to think about it, but it was affecting nearly everyone she knew. Her students were planning on moving. Businesses were closing or trying to figure out how to deal with the loss of customers.

Unfortunately, there wasn't much Holly could do about it. She was just a second grade teacher.

Snow fell in big flakes on the small car as they made their way up and into the Rocky Mountains. Heat blasted out of the vents, but it was still cold in the old car and Holly was glad she'd worn a sweater. Frost formed on the edges of the windows as they crossed over the continental divide. The trees disappeared at tree-line, giving the two women a clear view of the rocky tops of the mountains and miles of gray clouds.

Winter was heavy in the mountains as they crested the top of the pass and descended toward the ski slopes. White snow drifts stood high on the side of the two lane highway as tall evergreens came back to line the road. The car engine didn't whine on the way down like it did on the way up.

Slowly the gray faded into black and the mountains disappeared into the darkness of night. Snow drifted in hypnotizing patterns in front of the headlights, dancing around the car and back into the trees.

"Almost there," Aliyah announced just as Holly finished grading her last page. She was rather proud of her students. They'd all done the assignment and done well. It made her glad that they were learning.

Holly raised her eyes, scanning the snowy mountain road for the ski resort. As a native Coloradan, Holly had been skiing nearly every winter of her life, but the Blue Aspen Ski Resort was always way out of her price range. The lift ticket prices were higher than any other resort, and the hotel price might as well cost her entire teaching paycheck.

Blue Aspen was a place for A-list actors and billionaires to come play in the snow. The skiing was always said to be superb, but the hotel was the main attraction. It was supposedly a winter wonderland of comfort. Holly had only seen pictures of it in fancy magazines.

But today, Holly and Aliyah were going to get to experience it for themselves.

"ARE YOU DONE WORKING NOW?" Aliyah asked, turning off the highway and following the signs for the resort. "You promised you would use this as a vacation."

"I finished." Holly held up her school folder and tucked it

back into her bag. "I'm ready for our weekend adventure. No work, just play."

She leaned over and turned up the Christmas carols on the radio. Only a couple of weeks remained until Christmas. Holly was already signed up to help with the town parade and the Christmas Party at her dad's bookstore. The spirit of Christmas was slowly starting to infuse her soul.

"Good. We won this trip and we both need to just relax." Aliyah peered through the dark to check a road sign. "No work."

"No work. Promise." Holly held up three fingers like a scout.

"You weren't a scout, but I'm going to trust you on this." Aliyah gave Holly a serious look as she turned onto a smaller road. Snow drifted around a beautiful rock sign emblazoned with the Blue Aspen logo. They were almost to the resort.

The car came around a bend and both Aliyah and Holly gasped.

It looked like something on a Christmas card. If Holly were younger, she would have sworn they'd been magically transported to the North Pole and were about to visit Santa.

Tall peaked roofs dusted with snow glowed under white Christmas lights. The windows sparkled with fireplaces inside. Trees sparkled with lights and decorations. Everything was classy and contemporary. No blow-up decorations or plastic figurines, just the careful placement of lights and reflective ball ornaments.

It was absolutely stunning and magical.

Aliyah parked the car and turned off the engine. The car's cabin instantly dropped several degrees and they hurried to grab their bags from the back and head inside.

The inside of the resort was just as beautiful as the outside. Warm wood furniture filled the lobby. A giant fireplace glowed with flames. Candles flickered in nooks and on tables, while the scent of snow and fresh-baked cookies filled the air. A giant Christmas tree decorated with red satin streamers and fake snow stood proud in the center of the room.

"Wow," Aliyah whispered as they walked wide-eyed through the lobby to the check-in desk. "This is nice."

"Yeah."

"Welcome to the Blue Aspen Resort and Spa," the woman at the front desk greeted them with a smile. "How can I help you?"

"Hi. I'm Aliyah Jameson and this is Holly Jones. We have a reservation." Aliyah smiled at the woman as they set their bags down on the floor. "Holly won the Educator's Award."

"Of course." The woman quickly typed something into the computer. "Here you are."

Holly grinned at Aliyah. This was going to be great.

"You'll be staying in one of our premium suites." The woman handed them two plastic key-cards with mountains engraved into them. "These are your room keys as well as your lift tickets. You also have equipment rentals through our rental shop. You can pick up your gear any time tomorrow morning."

Holly slipped the key into her back pocket.

"Breakfast starts in the main dining room at five in the morning and goes until eleven," the woman continued. "The gym is on the third level with the spa. You also have access to the main pools and the network of hot springs pools around the resort. Your keys will let you into those areas as well. You can reserve any of the private ponds here or online."

"Network of hot springs?" Aliyah asked, her brow crinkling.

"Yes," the woman replied with a nod. "Blue Aspen Resort has a natural hot spring. There are several pools and private soaking ponds throughout the resort. They all interconnect and combine into the main pool just outside. It gives us a naturally heated outdoor pool."

Aliyah's jaw dropped open. "That's awesome."

The woman smiled at her and slid an envelope across the desk. "These are your tickets to the Educator's Award Ceremony tomorrow evening. The dress is formal."

"We already have a hair appointment booked," Holly informed her. Holly was going all out for this party. She even had a fancy designer dress that she'd borrowed from a friend.

"Excellent. If you need anything, please don't hesitate to let me know. Please enjoy your stay here at Blue Aspen." The woman smiled at both of them. "Do you need any assistance with your bags?"

"I think we're okay. Thank you," Holly replied. She bent over and picked up her duffle bag full of snow gear. Beside her, Aliyah did the same, but groaned slightly with the motion. Holly figured her friend was just sore from being in a car for three hours.

Holly turned and nearly ran directly into a man in a dark wool peacoat.

"Oh, I'm so sorry," she said quickly, stepping back and nearly into Aliyah. Holly's eye widened as she took in the expensive suit under the expensive jacket. She didn't recognize him as a celebrity, but then she wasn't exactly up to date on all the newest stars.

He certainly was handsome enough to be a celebrity.

"No harm," the man replied with a smile. His eyes were warm and dark. Holly blushed and quickly stepped out of the way. Aliyah was already halfway to the elevators when Holly caught up with her.

"Did you see that guy?" Holly asked her, glancing back at the man.

"No," Aliyah replied, shaking her head. She pressed the

elevator button twice in rapid succession and it miraculously appeared.

"Huh." Holly looked at the man one last time before stepping onto the elevator. She started to grin.

This was going to be an amazing trip.

$\mathcal{M}$erryweather

THINGS WERE LOOKING UP.

There were possibilities for love popping up all over the place. All it took was a little magic.

Merryweather felt rather than saw those possibilities when she watched Holly bump into Nathan. Love was written all over their futures.

It just needed a little push.

That was Merryweather's specialty.

CHAPTER 3

*N*athan

NATHAN'S PHONE buzzed like an angry hornet on the leather seat. Nathan didn't even glance at it. He kept his eyes on the road. Snow flurries danced in front of his headlights as he sped along the dark road toward the ski resort.

The heated seats kept him more than comfortable. The engine hummed with power as he shifted into a lower gear to accelerate up the mountain road. Behind him, two black SUVs struggled to keep pace with his silver all-wheel drive Ferrari.

The phone continued to buzz and he continued to ignore it as he focused on speed and taking the turns. He pushed harder, taking the icy turns just a little bit faster. The car slid, but he stayed in control.

He was on vacation now and there was no way he was going to let anyone ruin that for him.

It had been a rough month. He needed this.

He took the corner and the ski resort came into view. It was only then that he stopped driving like a madman. Blue Aspen Resort and Spa was one of his favorite places to ski. He'd skied nearly every continent, yet Blue Aspen Resort always felt like home. He loved the powder on the mountain and the warmth of the hot springs. Just driving up and seeing the resort entrance lowered his blood pressure.

Nathan swung his Ferrari into the valet parking and stepped out. The sun had set and the snow was coming down in big fat flakes that stuck to his hair. He took a deep breath in of icy air and smiled.

The two SUVs squealed into the valet line behind him. From the passenger side came a very large, and very angry looking man. He looked a little pale and clammy.

"Told you the Ferrari would handle just fine," Nathan told the man with a shrug, striking a nonchalant pose leaning against his car.

Gregory glared at Nathan as he approached. "That was not fun."

"Hal's an excellent driver. He managed that pass like a champ." Nathan couldn't help but grin. He'd pushed his Ferrari to the limit on speed through the mountain pass. The two SUVs with his personal security had struggled to keep up.

Gregory stood in front of Nathan, glaring down. Nathan wasn't a short man, but standing next to Gregory, he certainly felt like one. Gregory was nearly seven feet of pure muscle and strength. Nathan was fairly sure Gregory could kill a man with a single finger. Special Forces tended to teach those kinds of skills.

"You ride with Hal next time then," Gregory told him. "That was awful. I hate it when you drive like that."

Nathan grinned up at his bodyguard. "You said the

Ferrari couldn't handle it. I just needed to show you that it could."

"No, you just wanted to push the limits," Gregory replied. He shook his head like a tired parent. He sighed. "You need a coat."

Nathan chuckled and reached into the car. He pulled out a long wool peacoat and slid it over his shoulders. "Happy?"

Gregory didn't look amused.

"Let's go check in," Nathan said with a grin. He tossed his keys to the valet and headed inside. This was on of the few places that Gregory let him lead. The security risk was low here. It was another perk of staying in Blue Aspen. They were used to keeping celebrities and wealthy patrons safe and comfortable.

Nathan stepped inside and admired the Christmas decorations. He'd had his house in upstate New York mimic the style here: warm and contemporary. No gaudiness, just elegance. He didn't have a tree, though. He didn't see the point.

Two women stood at the check-in desk speaking with the receptionist. Nathan knew he could waltz up and demand service, but he didn't feel the need to be a dick. Besides, it sounded like they were nearly done.

He took a position a respectful distance away from the desk where it would be apparent he was next in line.

"Excellent. If you need anything, please don't hesitate to let me know. Please enjoy your stay here at Blue Aspen." The receptionist smiled at both of them. "Do you need any assistance with your bags?"

"I think we're okay. Thank you," replied the woman with a dirty-blonde ponytail. She bent over and picked up her duffle bag, swinging it over her shoulder.

And then turned and walked directly into him.

He wasn't used to not being seen. Nathan was usually the

center of attention everywhere he went. She looked up at him, her green eyes going wide.

"Oh, I'm so sorry," she said quickly, stepping back and just barely avoiding running into her friend.

"No harm," he replied, chuckling to himself. She was pretty, with freckles across her nose and dotting her cheeks. They were nearly obscured by the blush quickly filling her cheeks, but they were still there. He found he rather liked them.

The woman quickly hurried off, following her friend to the elevators. Nathan chuckled to himself. Although the woman was embarrassed, she didn't know who he was or she didn't care. If she had cared, she would have said something. Or grabbed her friend and at least giggled.

The truth was, he was the CEO of Paradigm Technologies and a billionaire.

Another perk of Blue Aspen was that his celebrity status didn't matter. Everyone was a celebrity here, even if they weren't. He wondered if maybe she was an actress or a model, but not a traditional one. She was on the shorter side and definitely nowhere near Hollywood skinny. She was definitely pretty enough, though.

"Good evening. I'm here to check in," Nathan said, walking up to the counter.

"Of course, Mr. Reed. We have your usual suite prepared to your specifications. There's a bottle of Dom Perignon chilling in the foyer as our gift to you." The receptionist smiled and slid a card across the desk for him. "Is there anything I can send up for you?"

Nathan pocketed the card. "No, thank you."

The woman smiled as Nathan turned around. His security team was already bringing in his things. They would have the smaller rooms adjacent to his. The warmth of the lodge finally permeated the wool of his coat and he took it off, carefully folding it over his arm.

"You left your phone in the car." Gregory handed him the phone. Six new calls.

"You know you could have just thrown it in a snowbank," Nathan told him. "I'm not talking to them."

Gregory chuckled. "I know. But it's fun to watch the veins on your neck pop out every time it rings."

"I thought you were supposed to be watching out for me," Nathan replied. "That's not watching out for me."

"No, that's just watching you," Gregory replied. "I've got to get my kicks somehow."

"You're a terrible bodyguard," Nathan said, putting the phone in the pocket of his jacket.

"Yeah, but you'd be dead and bored without me."

Nathan shook his head slowly as they walked to the elevators together. "Remind me to fire you later. Or at least dock your pay."

"I'll get right on that." Gregory checked the elevator before Nathan got on.

Nathan had no intention of firing Gregory. If anything, he'd give the man a raise. Gregory was more friend than employee at this point.

The phone buzzed and danced in Nathan's pocket. He reached in, hit the button and put it to his ear. It was Lucy, his secretary.

"What?" It came out a little harsher than he intended.

"RentTech," Lucy said without preamble. "Nathan, I have news on RentTech."

RentTech was Paradigm Technologies latest acquisition. As CEO, it was Nathan's idea to purchase the small company, but unfortunately, RentTech was turning into a money pit. Nothing seemed to go right. The board of directors for Paradigm was not pleased with their CEO or RentTech.

"I can fix it," he told her. "They just need a little more time-"

"Nathan." Lucy's voice was firm as she cut him off. "The board sold it this morning. RentTech's gone."

Nathan staggered slightly, his hand going to the wall to support him. "What?"

"That's why I've been calling you," Lucy explained. "I know you're on vacation this week, but you deserved to know. RentTech is gone."

"Damn it." He slammed his hand hard on the wall. All the work these past few months. He'd put everything into fixing RentTech and making it a successful part of Paradigm Technologies. Granted, there had been precious little success. RentTech was a disaster.

"I'm sorry, boss," Lucy said gently. "I know how much this meant to you. I know you put your reputation on the line for this."

Nathan closed his eyes and counted to five. "Well. It's done then. Time to work on something else."

"Enjoy your weekend," Lucy said. "I have things ready for the next company we've purchased. It's Elements Computer Technologies. I already did the legwork while you focused on RentTech. This next one will be a success. Promise."

Nathan nodded. He owed Lucy big for this. He'd focused all his energies on trying to salvage RentTech even when the board said to drop it. Lucy had managed his other responsibilities for him in the mean time. Things like preparing for another company to join Paradigm's umbrella.

"Thanks, Lucy." Nathan sighed.

"Just give me a good bonus later," she told him. "Have fun at your party tomorrow."

She clicked the line off and Nathan stood staring at his phone.

He'd failed. He should have felt devastated. Crushed.

And he did, but there was also a relief. No more stupid inane meetings. No more frantic emails that everyone else seemed to ignore. Sometimes he wished he didn't have this job. But then that would mean the money would stop. He couldn't let that happen. Money was everything.

He used to create technology. That was how he'd gotten into the tech world. Why Paradigm had hired him all those years ago. He'd risen to the top of the company, but he didn't create or innovate technology anymore. Now, he just managed it. It was starting to drain on him.

"You okay?" Gregory asked. Nathan had forgotten the man was still there.

"Fine."

Gregory grunted.

"What?" Nathan asked as the doors opened. Grunts were an entire language for Gregory.

"You're not fine," Gregory said. "You look like you need a drink."

"RentTech. It's gone." That's all Nathan needed to say.

Gregory grunted again.

Nathan looked over at him. "What? Tell me."

"You really want my opinion?" Gregory asked him. He checked the hallway before letting Nathan off the elevator. The suite door was open with Hal standing in front of it. That meant Hal had checked it and it was safe.

"I do," Nathan told him as they both entered the suite. Hal stayed outside by the door.

"The RentTech mess was awful," Gregory said simply. "The sale to Paradigm was always about the money, not the company. It was a bad match. It wasn't for you. You did everything you could. The board gave you a shitty job."

That was basically the opinion Nathan had come to himself about the rocky results of the company purchase. It was good to hear someone else say it. "Why do you say that?"

"The past month has been hellish working for you. It's made you short-tempered. You're unhappy. You're exhausted." Gregory shrugged. "These aren't good things for you."

"Yeah, but RentTech was supposed to make me a lot of money," Nathan countered. "It would have been worth it."

"Says you," Gregory replied. "It didn't look worth it from where I'm standing."

Nathan sighed. Money was always worth it. Money was everything.

"My advice to you is to take this weekend. No work. Don't talk about it, don't think about it," Gregory said. "Give yourself a break."

"That's kind of the plan," Nathan replied.

"You say that, but then you work." Gregory crossed his arms and looked at Nathan. "You always work and it makes you miserable."

"What do you mean?" Nathan went to the bottle of Dom and popped the cork. He offered the bottle to Gregory, but the bodyguard shook his head. He was working.

"I don't want you to take this the wrong way, Boss," Gregory said slowly. "When you deal with RentTech, you're short tempered. You don't joke with the boys. You don't smile as much. That week the board made someone else handle things, you wouldn't stop whistling and humming. Drove poor Hal bonkers."

Nathan poured himself a glass of champagne and sipped thoughtfully. "It drove Hal bonkers?"

"You were off key. The guy has perfect pitch."

Nathan chuckled.

"I'll try not to hum this time."

Gregory grunted again.

"What?"

"Don't do this again." Gregory frowned. "You work too

hard. You need a girl. Or a guy. But someone. You need more in your life than just work and money."

That was more work advice than Nathan had ever heard from Gregory. The man must really be worried about him.

"Here." Nathan handed Gregory his phone.

"What do you want me to do with this?" Gregory asked. The phone looked tiny in Gregory's massive hands.

"Throw it in a snowbank. Give it to the less fortunate. Melt it down and make art. I don't care." A sense of freedom started to wash through him. "It's my weekend off."

Gregory set the phone on the ground and stomped it with his heel. The entire thing shattered.

"Wow. I didn't think you were going to take me literally." Nathan took another sip of champagne. "I feel better already."

Gregory grunted.

This time, Nathan just shook his head and poured another glass of champagne. He was definitely on vacation now.

CHAPTER 4

*H*olly

"Is that your stomach?" Holly asked. A low grumble filled the elevator.

Aliyah shifted her feet uncomfortably. "Yeah."

"Are you okay?" Holly asked. Beads of sweat popped out on Aliyah's forehead and she looked pale. Her beautiful skin was usually a rich milk chocolate, but right now, she looked like she'd been Photoshopped into black and white.

"My stomach," Aliyah whispered. She swallowed hard and stared at the elevator buttons, willing the elevator to get to their floor faster.

When the silver doors opened, Aliyah bolted, leaving behind her bags as she sprinted down the hallway. Holly put Aliyah's bag over her shoulder and followed behind at a much more human pace.

"Wow," Holly said, coming in the front door of their hotel room.

It was bigger than her apartment.

The style was elegant western. Wood furniture with rustic accents decorated the living room, but the main appeal was the huge windows overlooking the ski slope. It was too dark to see the full view, but Holly could tell it would be impressive in the morning.

The bathroom door to Holly's right slammed shut and Holly could hear Aliyah inside. It did not sound like a pleasant time.

"You okay?" Holly called through the door.

Aliyah just moaned and Holly shook her head.

"I'll put your stuff in the room," Holly told her, shouldering both bags and heading to the bedroom.

Two queen beds took up the bedroom facing a huge flat screen TV. The bed frames were wooden and heavy. The beds looked warm with thick down comforters. The pillows were soft and fluffy. Holly could barely wait to crawl into bed and snuggle down into the soft sheets.

She set their bags down, one on each bed. She opened her bag and pulled out her toiletry kit to put in the bathroom.

The master bath was huge. There was a big shower with two shower heads and a steam control function, but it was the tub that caught Holly's attention. A big, beautiful soaking tub. It was deep and long enough that she could stay submerged sitting or laying down. She wouldn't have to choose between having cold shoulders or cold knees.

She was already planning on a long bubble-bath at least once this trip.

Holly grabbed some pink stomach pills from her toiletry kit and headed back to the living room. She could still hear Aliyah loosing her dinner in the bathroom. She tapped gently on the door.

"Medicine," she called.

"It's open," croaked Aliyah.

Holly cautiously pushed open the door. As an elementary school teacher, she'd seen her share of barf. It wasn't her favorite thing, but she could handle it.

Aliyah looked miserable. Her dark hair hung limp around her pale-green face. "I don't feel so good. I think the sandwich was a bad idea."

Holly held out the pink tablets. "Here. I'll go get you some ginger ale from downstairs. You want anything else?"

"A new body," Aliyah groaned. "Or a time machine."

"I'll see what they have at the market."

Aliyah began worshiping the porcelain god once again and Holly quickly escaped. She took the elevator to the lobby, figuring that there had to be a small convenience store there. There were always small shops with overpriced aspirin bottles and expensive energy drinks in hotels.

The fire in the lobby fireplace crackled and danced as she came down. Everything was warm and cheery. Soft holiday music played overhead and the smell of fresh-baked cookies still filled the air. The receptionist looked busy checking in new guests, so Holly decided to explore on her own. She followed the scent of the cookies, hoping they would lead to baking rather than a scented candle.

The scent came from real cookies on the end of a bar. She didn't get one, instead going for a drink. Two stainless steel drums etched with mountain scenes sat on the counter next to the cookies. Big heavy mugs waited next to the containers. Holly glanced around before taking a mug and pouring some liquid out from one of the containers. It was hot chocolate, the real kind, not the mix. Holly sighed with pleasure, filled up her mug the rest of the way, and took a sip.

It wasn't the ginger ale she'd promised Aliyah, but she wasn't going to say no to hot chocolate.

She moved down the bar, peering over the counter and

looking around. She hoped to find some sort of drink fountain.

"You looking for something?" a male voice asked.

Holly spun, nearly spilling her drink all over the speaker. She managed to keep it all in her cup, which she was grateful for. It was the man she'd run into at check-in. The last thing she needed was to spill hot chocolate all over him as well.

"I'm actually trying to find some ginger ale," Holly explained. "I didn't want to bother anyone."

The man smiled. He no longer wore the suit. Now it was comfortable sweat pants and a long-sleeved t-shirt. His brown eyes looked more relaxed and he smiled easily at her.

"There's a drink station over here," he explained, pointing to the other end of the bar. Tucked behind a potted plant was a traditional soda dispenser with cups and lids stacked neatly beside it.

"Thank you." Holly hurried over and filled a cup with ginger ale. She smiled at the man. "I really appreciate it."

He shrugged. "No problem. Your first time here?"

Holly nodded. "Yup."

And probably her last. There was no way she'd be able to afford to come back here. Even though she was enjoying it, she knew it was way out of her price range.

"Be sure to try the waffles at breakfast," the man advised. "They put just a hint of orange in them. They're amazing."

Holly grinned. "Thank you. Waffles are my favorite breakfast food. I'll be sure to get some."

The man smiled and gave her a wave before picking up his own drink cup and heading back to the elevators.

Holly watched him go, trying not to stare at his butt. The sweatpants accentuated the muscle underneath and told her that the man did not skip leg day.

"Aliyah would tell me to get his number," Holly said to

herself. She nearly went after the handsome man, but held back. She needed to take care of her friend. Maybe she'd run into the man again tomorrow over waffles.

It was possible.

CHAPTER 5

$\mathscr{H}$olly

HOLLY STRETCHED out in the soft bed and sighed with contentment. There was something magical about not waking up to the sound of an alarm clock. She snuggled into the fluffy comforter for a moment, enjoying the dark silence of the hotel room.

Then she remembered that she was going skiing today. With a grin, she threw back the covers and got out of bed. The floors were heated and she nearly moaned with delight. She'd gotten so used to keeping her apartment cold to keep the heating bill down, she'd forgotten how nice it was to wake up and be warm.

In the next bed over, Aliyah slept. She still looked pale, but better than the death-warmed-over look she had last night. The poor thing had spent most of the night in the bathroom dealing with the aftermath of food poisoning.

No more gas station sandwiches for either of them.

Holly tip-toed to the bathroom and enjoyed the heated tile floors in there. If she ever built a house of her own design, heated tile floors in the bathroom were definitely on the list. It felt amazing to have warm feet while she brushed her teeth and put on her ski clothes. She put her hair up in a ponytail and quietly left the bathroom.

"Hey." Aliyah's voice was hoarse and sounded painful.

"Hey. Did I wake you up?" Holly asked, pausing by the bathroom door.

"No, I've been awake for a few minutes. Believe it or not, I didn't sleep great last night."

"I'm sorry," Holly replied.

"Not your fault." Aliyah shifted around on the bed. "You going skiing?"

"Yeah. Are you going to come? How are you feeling?"

"I'm going to stay in bed all day. And maybe the tub. I think I can handle a bath," Aliyah said. "I'm no longer puking my guts out, but I don't want to move more than the four feet to the bathroom."

"Can I get you anything?" She hated that her best friend wasn't feeling well. They were supposed to spend the day out in the snow having fun. Instead, her friend was going to stay inside being sick.

"More of that ginger ale would be great. I'm sorry I can't ski with you today."

"Me too." Holly pouted and shrugged. "But, at least if you're going to be sick, this is the place. The toilets are all clean and you don't have to clean up after."

Aliyah chuckled. "Yeah. And they have cable here. And HBO. I'm watching *Game of Thrones* all day today."

"Don't spoil anything for me," Holly replied. She crossed the room and put her pajamas in her suitcase.

"They all die," Aliyah told her. "Even the dragons."

"LA LA LA, I CAN'T HEAR YOU," Holly shouted, putting

her hands over her ears. She then stuck her tongue out at Aliyah.

Aliyah lay back on her pillows. "You should get going. It's almost time for the lifts to start. Got to get that fresh powder."

"Okay. I'm going to go grab some breakfast and hit the slopes. I'll bring you back some ginger ale. You want any food?"

Aliyah turned a little green at the mention of food. She shook her head. "I'll order room service if I get hungry."

Holly nodded and waved before heading downstairs. She followed the scent of waffles to the dining area. The room was comfortably full, with enough open chairs that she didn't have to wait, but not so empty that she felt strange eating alone.

The waffles were amazing, just as the man had said the night before. Holly ate two and sipped at a large mug of coffee. Outside the big windows snow started to fall. Holly grinned. It would be a good powder day.

She finished her breakfast and hurried a huge cup of ginger ale up to Aliyah. She'd already fallen back asleep with the sounds of a dragon battle raging through the TV. The fact that she was sleeping through the best parts of the show told Holly that Aliyah still didn't feel well.

Holly left the soda on the nightstand, grabbed the rest of her snow gear, and headed down to the rental shop.

The rental shop was just off the south end of the lobby. Holly stepped inside and filled out her waivers and insurance information.

"Hi. Welcome to the Ski Shoppe," the woman behind the counter said, taking her paperwork. "Are you skiing or snowboarding?"

"Skiing." Holly wanted to learn how to snowboard, but she knew she'd need lessons. That was something she wasn't really able to afford on her teacher's salary. Especially not at a place like Blue Aspen.

"Excellent choice," the woman told her. She hopped off a stool behind the counter, and Holly realized that the woman was much shorter than Holly had first thought. She also couldn't put an age on the woman. Her face said she was early twenties, but there was a wisdom in her lavender eyes that said she was much, much older. Also, her hair was so blonde it was silver. Not gray, but actually silver. "I'm Merryweather."

"It's nice to meet you, Merryweather," Holly replied. "Thank you for helping me."

"It's my pleasure." The woman's lavender eyes sparkled. She handed Holly a pair of boots to try on. "I love this time of year, don't you?"

Holly smiled and nodded as she slid on the boots. They fit perfectly. Usually she had to try on a couple of pairs, but these felt like they were made for her. "I love Christmas. There's something magical about it"

"Yes, there most certainly is." Merryweather grinned at her and took one of the boots. She fitted it to a ski and hummed while she made some adjustments. "Have you experienced any Christmas magic yet this season?"

"Just this trip," Holly replied. "I think it used up most of my luck quota for the rest of the year."

Merryweather looked up at her and smiled with those ageless eyes. "I don't know. I think you might have more Christmas magic in store."

Before Holly had a chance to answer, Merryweather handed her the skis, poles, and a helmet.

"These are the same kind of skis the US Olympic team uses, so be sure to wear the helmet," Merryweather reminded her. "Plus, it's hotel policy."

Holly believed this equipment was made for professionals. Everything was top of the line. The boots fit like they were made for her. The poles didn't feel too long or too short, and she couldn't wait to take the skis out for a run. They looked like they'd handle the turns like a dream.

"Thank you, Merryweather," Holly said, trying to balance everything and mostly managing.

"Have a great day. I'm sure I'll see you again soon." The silver-haired woman waved and Holly left.

Outside, snow flurries danced and dusted the ski resort with a fresh layer of powder. The air was cold and crisp, smelling of snow and pine. Holly put on her snow pants and ski jacket, making sure the key card was in the front pocket. It was the pocket with a small bunny embroidered on it. She put it there so she wouldn't forget where it was later.

She put on her gloves and her bunny goggles. One of her students had given the goggles to her as a gift several years ago. They had a cute little bunny sticker on the top corner that matched the one on her jacket. She also had a green fleece scarf with cute little cottontail bunnies and Christmas trees wrapped around her neck to keep her face warm. Another gift from her students.

Apparently, they thought she liked bunnies.

With a grin so big it made her face feel like bursting, she snapped on her skis and headed to the lift. The sun peeked out from behind a cloud, making the world explode in color. Tiny ice crystals sparkled in the air. It was like being inside a glitter snow-globe.

Holly was late out to the lifts, which was fine by her. There was hardly any line now and she would probably get to ride up by herself.

That was until she heard a deep voice from behind her.

"Mind if I ride up with you?"

CHAPTER 6

$\mathcal{M}$*erryweather*

THINGS WERE GOING WELL, Merryweather thought to herself. She busied herself behind the Ski Shoppe counter, making sure things were just so. She liked it when things were how they were supposed to be.

She looked out and watched as the man found his way to the lift.

The smile between them told Merryweather she was on the right track, but that they needed more time.

Well, that just meant that Merryweather had to use some magic. She'd start small.

Something to keep them talking. Something to give them the time they needed to find the love within them.

CHAPTER 7

*H*olly

HOLLY TURNED to see the man from last night. Or at least, she was pretty sure it was him. It was hard to be sure with the dark sunglasses over his eyes.

Either way her stomach did an excited flip-flop. The guy was cute.

"Sure!" she said, sounding maybe a little more excited than she should have. Together they glided out after a ski chair and waited for the next one to pick them up. Holly was grateful she managed to sit down on the chairlift seat gracefully. She only clattered her poles a little.

Once seated, she glanced over at her companion. He wore a black expensive looking ski-jacket with matching snow pants, gloves, and helmet. Everything looked brand new. He wore skis and had traces of snow already covering his tips.

He hadn't been late to the lifts.

"How's the snow?" Holly asked as the lift chugged forward.

"Amazing," the man replied. "But then, it always is here. I'm fairly sure they have a magic super power to make the best snow here. I've never had a bad day."

"So you come here often?" He certainly looked wealthy enough to afford skiing here.

"As often as I can. It's usually only once or twice a year, though. You?"

"This is my first time," Holly replied honestly. "I'm loving it so far."

"Did you try the waffles?" the man asked.

So it *was* him. Holly grinned and felt a little flutter in her stomach. He remembered her. Somehow, that made her feel important.

"I did. They were just as good as you said they would be. Thank you for the recommendation. Anything else I should try?"

The man pursed his lips thoughtfully for a moment and Holly immediately thought of kissing him. She shook herself, surprised at how easily the thought had come.

"If you stay for dinner, the prime rib is spectacular," he said after a moment. He smiled at her. "How long are you staying?"

The giddy flutter in her stomach returned and she was glad her scarf covered her face so he wouldn't see the blush.

"I'm just here for the weekend. We leave on Sunday."

"We?"

Holly wondered if the hint of unhappiness she heard in his voice was all in her head. It had been a while since she'd flirted with someone. At least here on the chairlift, she had a captive audience if her flirting was rusty.

"My friend and I," Holly quickly explained. "She's like a sister to me. We work together."

The man's smile returned. "Ah. What do you do?"

"I'm a teacher. What about you?"

"I run a business," the man replied with a shrug.

"That sounds interesting," Holly said, shifting the ski poles to rest under her leg a little more comfortably.

"Depends on the day." He glanced around at the beautiful snow covered landscape around them. "I think today's a good day."

Holly giggled. She had to agree. The sun shimmered down through a cascade of icy glitter. White snow frosted the dark green evergreens and coursed like frozen streams down the mountain sides. One mountain rose up before them, the lift carrying them up to the highest reaches, while others stood proud and snow-capped as far as the eye could see.

Suddenly, the lift came to a halt. Holly and the man hung suspended in midair for a moment, rocking gently. They hung at least fifty feet from the ground, suspended over firs and pines.

"Someone must have fallen off the lift trying to get on," Holly said, trying to peer up the mountain to see the top. They appeared to be in the middle of the ride.

"I did see some private lessons getting on before us," the man agreed. It was common for the lifts to stop whenever people fell getting on or off the lifts, and the newbies in lessons were usually the culprits. It took practice to ride a ski lift.

They both sat there for a moment, waiting for the lift to start back up again. Stops and starts were common, but they were usually short.

This one lasted longer than usual. The sun disappeared behind a bank of clouds, casting the world into gray shadows.

"Think they'll bring us hot chocolate if they can't get it started again?" Holly asked.

He chuckled and took off his sunglasses. The warmth of his brown eyes made the loss of sun bearable. "I hope so. Maybe a good book, too."

"Nonfiction or fiction?"

He turned and faced her. "On vacation? Fiction. Before bed, non-fiction."

"Why non-fiction before bed?"

"I like the fiction books too much. I won't sleep. I have to know what the next chapter is. Does the dragon devour the town? Do the aliens win? How does the pauper become a prince? What about you?" the man asked. "Fiction or non-fiction?"

"Fiction. I am a sucker for a good romance. And Dr. Seuss, of course, but that's more on a professional level."

The man laughed, the rich sound echoing off the snowy mountain tops. Holly found her heart speeding up and she was glad to be stuck on this chairlift with him. At this point, she didn't really care if they stayed up here forever.

The lift stayed still. Holly scraped her skis together, brushing off the little snow that rested on them.

"What are you reading right now?" Holly asked. "Anything good?"

"I'm between books at the moment. Have any recommendations?"

"Other than Dr. Seuss?" Holly grinned at him.

The man chuckled again, flashing her that great smile. "I can always have more rhymes in my life."

"There's so many good ones," Holly said thoughtfully. "At my dad's bookstore, I'm always scoping out new books."

"I hope you get a family discount," the man replied.

"If I did, he'd go broke." She smiled, but inside she felt her chest tighten. Her dad's bookstore wasn't doing so well.

Another casualty of everyone leaving town. Even without her discount, he really was going broke.

Unfortunately, it was then that the chairlift started to move. Their time was up. The man put his glasses back down, covering his eyes.

"No mountain-side hot chocolate for us," Holly teased him, hoping to make him laugh again.

"Maybe next time. You can give me your book recommendations then."

The lift sped up and the wind blew cold on Holly's face. She tucked her chin into her Christmas bunny scarf. The top of the mountain loomed into view along with the end of the lift. Part of her was sad because she'd enjoyed the company, but another part was excited. It was time to ski.

"Have a good run, Snow-bunny," the man said as the lift came to the end. At her confused look, he pointed to her scarf.

She chuckled and together they both stood and exited the chair. He went to the left, she went to the right. She was sad to see him go. It had been wonderful to talk about books with him. Plus, it totally counted as flirting. Aliyah would be proud of her.

She took a deep breath of mountain air. She was determined to have fun, just like Aliyah recommended. She would use this ski day and party to take her mind off things at home. It would be just the break she needed.

With a deep breath and a grin hidden by her scarf, Holly started down the mountain.

Icy wind with fat flakes rushed past her as she picked up speed. She swooshed and slid down the hillside. The skis were amazing. She truly did feel like an Olympic skier with this equipment. For the first time in her life, she thought that she might have a chance at a gold medal.

That was until a woman in a racing suit blew past her on a straight-away.

Still, Holly enjoyed the sensation of being a good skier, even if she wasn't quite ready for the time-trials just yet.

Once back at the bottom of the mountain, Holly slid back into the line for the lift. Maybe on the next run she'd go across the mountain and take the lift to the north side. The runs were harder over there, so she wanted to make sure that she felt comfortable on her skis before hitting the black diamonds.

"Well, hello again, Snow-bunny."

Holly turned to see the man standing beside her ready to go on the lift.

"We're going to have to stop running into one another like this," she teased as the chair swung around and they once again followed it out.

"What if I like running into you, Snow-bunny?" He flashed her a grin as they waited for the chair to come up behind them.

"You're such a charmer," she said once they were safely seated on the lift.

"Just call me Prince Charming," he replied with a laugh.

As they raised into the air and away from the ground, the sun came out once more.

"What run did you do?" he asked, settling himself on the chair. Tiny flecks of ice sparkled behind him, creating a halo effect.

"Dragon Tamer." She tilted her head as she looked at him. "Any runs you recommend?"

"They're all good. But my favorite is Lovely Lady. It's a black diamond, but it's more blue than black to be honest."

"I'll have to try it. Blue-blacks are my favorite kind of run. There's just enough challenge to make it fun. I usually go back to greens at the end of the day when I'm tired." She smiled at him. "Hopefully I can find one. This place is huge. I'm hoping I don't get lost."

"Would you like to join me? It's always nice to have company. You won't get lost that way."

A slow, warm heat filled her core as she smiled at him. Holly could only imagine how proud Aliyah would be of her for not only flirting, but actually hanging out with a cute male for the day. It was almost like going on a date.

"I'd love to. Thank you."

He grinned at her and the warm tingles continued all down her body. She didn't care that it was below freezing. She was heated by her inner fires.

"I'm Holly, by the way." She held out her gloved hand.

He took her glove in his and gave the closest approximation of a handshake they could with heavy winter gloves on. "Nathan."

She grinned.

Today just kept on getting better.

CHAPTER 8

*N*athan

HE WASN'T QUITE sure why he invited her to ski with him.

Maybe it was her smile. Maybe it was how easy it was to talk to her. Maybe he was lonely. Maybe it was the fact that she rocked the snow-bunny look.

Whatever the reason, he was glad he'd asked her.

They did three more runs, taking Lovely Lady twice and then Dragon Tamer. She kept pace with him easily. He was a decent skier and had taken lessons from some of the top names in the sport, yet she moved with an effortless grace that he admired.

Plus, the conversation on the lifts was the best he'd had in weeks. She didn't talk about mergers and expense reports. There was no mention of board members and equity payments.

Instead, they talked about books. Her tastes were wonderfully eclectic, ranging from romance to science fiction and then to political thrillers. It seemed there wasn't a book she hadn't read. They talked about plots and stories. They connected on characters and laughed about things they'd read.

It was one of the best conversations he'd had in a long time.

"Can I buy you lunch?" she asked as they finished their third run together. Her cheeks were flushed with the cold and exertion.

"You want to buy me lunch?" Nathan's eyebrows raised. Usually, he was the one making the offer of buying lunch. It came with having the title of billionaire. Everyone expected him to pay for things.

"Yeah." She shrugged. "My treat."

A warm wave of surprise washed over him. "Sure. What were you thinking?"

She bit her lower lip and smiled bashfully up at him. "I actually have no idea where we should eat. I'm just hungry. Those waffles were a long time ago."

He chuckled. "There's two options. The lodge has great sandwiches and burgers, or there's a restaurant at the top of the Kicking Horse Chairlift. It's got amazing views and the food is delicious."

She chewed on her bottom lip for a moment. "You know what? Go big or go home. Let's do the restaurant at the top." She grinned. "Race you to the lift."

She took off, moving her skis from side to side and using her poles to propel her forward. Nathan stayed back, enjoying watching the swing of her hips. He found her curves alluring. He usually dated waif-like models, but they left him unsatisfied.

Maybe he had been dating the wrong kind of woman.

They took the lift to the top of the mountain. The sun

played peek-a-boo behind the clouds, casting long shadows on the white powdery snow.

"Where now?" she asked, when they got off the lift.

"We go to Kicking Horse," Nathan replied. "This way."

He turned and took a path they hadn't taken yet. It went down the backside of the mountain. She kept up easily, her blonde hair streaming out behind her from under her helmet.

"Turn left, Snow-bunny," he called. She pivoted on her skis and took the turn, narrowly avoiding a clump of trees. He followed close behind her, chasing her with his speed.

She looked back at him and grinned, tucking her arms and bending her knees into a racing stance. She flew down one path, heading toward the now visible chair-lift. He was doing everything he could to pass her. She wasn't going to let him win, and he liked the competition.

On the last stretch to the lift, his extra weight gave him the edge. He finally managed to pass her, coming in first to stop at the entrance to the lift. She came in hot on his heels and did a hockey stop, blasting him with snow.

She took one look at him and doubled over in laughter. He had snow coating his entire front. She'd hit a perfect patch of powdered snow and managed to completely paint the front of him in white.

"Nice stop," he said, with a chuckle. He wiped his gloved hands over his glasses so that he could see again. He shook himself like a wet dog, but most of the snow stayed stuck to his jacket and ski-pants.

She reached out and carefully dusted some of the snow from his shoulders.

"You have a little something on you," she said, leaving the majority of the snow still resting on his head and chest.

He took the opportunity to grab some snow from the

drift behind him, turning it into a snowball. He threw it at her.

The snowball hit her helmet with a splat. He could see her eyes go wide in her ski-goggles before narrowing.

With a smooth motion, she used her poles to pop the bindings on her boots and freed herself from her skis. With her long skis no longer limiting her range of motion, she reached down, grabbed a snowball and threw it back at him.

It hit him square in the chest, simply adding to the snow already there.

He grinned. This meant war.

Nathan popped himself out of his skis, dropped his poles and retaliated with a well aimed snowball to her chest. She twisted, moving her body at the last second to avoid being hit, but he had a second one ready. She managed to miss that one as well.

"You think you can get me?" she teased, splattering a snowball against his arm. She'd managed to hit him twice now while seeming to avoid every snowball he threw at her. "I play dodge-ball on a regular basis. You're going to have to do better than that!"

He sent another ball of snow heading straight for her back, but once again she danced right out from under it.

Now it was time to get serious.

He reached down and made a perfect snowball. It was bigger than his fist and full of cold, white snow.

This time, he feinted throwing it, causing her to twist away. When no snowball came, she paused and he made his move. He sprinted the short distance between them and instead of throwing the ball, tackled her into a fluffy snow drift.

He then proceeded to put the snowball down the back of her jacket.

She yelped with the sudden cold, twisting and shaking

until she got the majority of the snow out of her coat. She glared at him for a second before breaking out into a grin. He smiled back at her, innocent as to her plan.

Then she pushed a snowball of her own down the front of his coat.

"Truce!" he spluttered, the cold turning wet and dripping down his front. He did his best to get the snow out, but some had melted. It was cold and wet.

"Truce." She chuckled. "Nice tackle."

"I played soccer in college," he replied. They lay there in the snow, gasping for breath. Soft snow began to fall, landing gently on their upturned faces. It was then that she started to giggle.

His own laughter bubbled up, breaking past the reserved business exterior and filling the mountain with their joy. He shook with laughter. The more he laughed, the harder she laughed until they were both laying on the ground, convulsing with giggles.

He lay there with her, stuck in a snow drift with snow down both their jackets, laughing like maniacs.

He hadn't laughed that hard in ages. It felt good. His soul felt light for the first time in years. To be honest, he couldn't remember laughing like that since childhood.

Slowly, they both regained their composure. He managed to get up to his feet in the deep snow before turning and offering her a hand.

He pulled her up, and she stumbled forward, her hands coming to his chest. Instinctively, his arms wrapped around her.

She looked up at him through long eyelashes, the pink in her cheeks darkening. Her lips were cherry red and his mouth watered to kiss her. He tipped his chin, moving in for a kiss. She lifted her face, her beautiful mouth moving to meet his.

And their helmets bonked with a hard plastic sound. There would be no easy kiss with their safety gear in place. The moment shifted, and the kiss was lost.

She giggled again, stepping out of his arms. "Lunch?"

He nodded and together they found their poles and skis. She clicked her boots into the skis and waited for him to do the same. Together, they worked their way to the where the chair-lift spun to pick up passengers.

The lift attendant looked them both over and slowly shook his head. He'd obviously seen their snowball fight and wasn't impressed. Nathan didn't care. He was having fun. The next chair came and the attendant motioned them forward and onto the next seat.

He glanced over to see her smiling at him as the chair bumped into the back of his legs and sped them into the sky. The snow fell hard around them, muffling the sound of the lift. She grinned at him, looking like something from a advertisement for the resort.

His chest tightened a little around his heart at her beauty. That smile. The way she made him laugh. A couple of hours with her, and he was smiling and laughing again.

He wondered what he would be like if she was always around her. He imagined he would be happy. She was some sort of winter magic.

"You still have some snow on your jacket," she teased, pointing to his shoulders. The dark jacket was still dusted with white from their snowball fight.

He nodded, reaching his hand up to brush it away. Only, instead of brushing it off, he brushed it in her direction. He made sure to flick as much snow as possible at her.

She threw her head back and laughed, holding up her hands to block his snowy attack.

He laughed too, feeling happy for the first time in ages.

CHAPTER 9

*N*athan

THE SNOW WAS FALLING HARD ENOUGH that the restaurant didn't have many patrons. It was on the top of a mountain. The only way to get to it was by chair-lift or a snowmobile. They practically had the place to themselves.

"Just wait until you try their hot chocolate. It's amazing," Nathan told her. "You'll love it."

"I can't wait," she replied with a grin. "I love hot chocolate. It's one of my favorite drinks in the whole world."

They left their skis outside and hung their jackets on a wooden peg inside the heavy front door. Warmth from multiple fireplaces made the room comfortable after the cold outside. Yet another Christmas tree sat in a position of honor. Nathan ignored it.

The restaurant was styled like an old log cabin. The furniture inside was rustic, but the windows were huge. The

46

hostess sat them at a small table in front of the main window overlooking the ski basin.

"Wow," Holly whispered. She sat staring out the window at the incoming storm over the craggy peaks. Dark clouds sat like unhappy hats on the tops of the mountains as snow fell, turning the dark green pine trees to white statues.

"It's a great view," he agreed, settling into his chair. He stretched his legs out under the table, wiggling his toes. They'd both loosened their boots and now the circulation was slowly returning to his feet.

"It's kind of what I imagine the North Pole looks like," Holly told him, her eyes still glued to the window.

"The North Pole?" Nathan wondered why she was thinking of the North Pole. This was more like Antarctica with the mountain ranges.

"Yeah. Like Santa," she said with a smile. She motioned to the Christmas tree behind him and it was then that he noticed the soft music overhead was actually instrumental versions of Christmas carols.

"Oh." He took a sip of his water and looked out the window.

"Wow. Not a Christmas fan, I take it?" She put her elbows on the table and cradled her chin in her hands.

"I like Christmas." He shrugged.

She raised her eyebrows. "Could have fooled me. Why don't you like it?"

"I don't know. I guess it's all so commercial. I stopped believing in Santa a long time ago."

"What about your family? Do you go visit them for the holidays?"

"Sometimes. I tend to be busy. We never really did much for Christmas after my younger brother learned the truth about Santa." He shrugged again. "I'll visit my brother and my dad after the new year. We're not big on the holiday."

She nodded. She took in everything about him and he wondered what she was thinking. He felt like she could read him, seeing all the unspoken lost and forgotten Christmases in his past.

"Let me guess, you like Christmas." He crossed his arms, watching her.

Holly's green eyes sparkled as she smiled. "I *love* Christmas. I know it's cliché, but it really is my favorite time of the year."

"Because of the presents?"

She shook her head, crinkling her nose. "No, not really. I mean, I love giving presents, and I love when someone makes me something special. My students tend to give me mugs and chocolates. I love those, even though I have more mugs than actual dishes in my house."

He couldn't help but smile at her upbeat attitude. "What about your family?"

"It's just me and my dad, but we love Christmas. We throw this big bash for the whole town on Christmas day. My students love it." She grinned, lost in memory. "My dad buys books and toys for all the local kids and then Dad dresses up like Santa. It's my favorite part of the holiday to see the kids all light up."

Her smile faltered slightly, as if something made her sad, but she shook herself and refocused on him. "If you're ever in Colorado for the holidays, you should come join us."

"I'll keep that in mind," he replied, knowing that he probably wouldn't. Christmas wasn't his thing. His family never really did much for the holiday other than make him feel guilty. Once he moved out of his father's house, he had started working through the Christmas holiday season. It was better that way.

A small tug of jealousy hit him. Holly looked forward to

Christmas. He dreaded it. He wished that he liked it more, but the Hallmark Christmas never happened for him.

It was usually full of people trying to get more money and better presents out of him. Somehow, everyone who became his friend expected expensive gifts since he was a billionaire. Granted, he did give lavish gifts, but the entitlement rubbed him the wrong way.

Plus, Christmas just never appealed to him. It was better to work. Better to earn money than waste it.

"I'm so sorry to keep you waiting," a waitress said, breaking into his thoughts. "What can I get you?"

"Menus," Nathan replied. He motioned to their bare table with a forgiving smile.

The waitress looked surprised. "I'm sorry about that." She hurried to the front reception area, glared at the hostess, and returned with two menus. "Our special today is rib-eye with our special mashed potatoes. The soup is clam chowder, and I have to tell you it's delicious."

"Oh, I love rib-eye," Holly said, cracking open her menu.

"While I let you look at the menu, can I get you any drinks?" the waitress asked.

Nathan glanced over at Holly, expecting to see her mouth watering as she looked at the menu. He knew the hot chocolate was on the first page. Instead she looked like she might be sick.

"Just water for me, please," Holly said quickly. Nathan frowned.

"What about the hot chocolate?" he asked her.

"Just water, please," Holly repeated to the waitress.

"Well, I'll take a hot chocolate," Nathan said. "And a glass of water, too, please."

The waitress smiled and nodded before heading off to the kitchen.

"You okay?" Nathan asked once the waitress was gone.

She swallowed hard as she looked at the menu. "Maybe we could just get drinks here, and food down at the lodge."

"But you only ordered water," Nathan reminded her.

"Right." Her forehead was creased and eyebrows drawn. "I'm actually not very hungry."

He seemed to remember her saying she was hungry when she asked him to lunch. What had changed?

"What's wrong?" he asked her, more gently this time. He reached out and touched her hand.

She pulled away, setting the menu down. She stayed quiet for a moment, shame painted clearly on her face.

"I know I said I'd buy lunch, but... I can't afford this." He almost didn't hear her she was so quiet. She smoothed her hair back and took a deep breath. Her green eyes wouldn't meet his. "I don't have enough money to pay for lunch here. It's too expensive."

Nathan sat speechless for a moment. He looked down at the menu and looked at the prices for the first time.

The hot chocolate was expensive. The rib-eye was absurdly marked up. Even just a simple side-salad cost more than a full meal at a regular steakhouse.

"I know I said I'd pay for lunch," Holly said, filling the silence. Her voice cracked slightly. "But, with Christmas in less than two weeks... and I don't get paid until the end of the month..."

Nathan felt like an idiot. He was the one who'd suggested the mountaintop restaurant. He looked over at Holly, seeing her well-worn sweater and lack of jewelry for the first time. Her jacket wasn't designer. Her snow-pants had a tear in the knee and didn't really match the jacket.

"Here's that hot chocolate," the waitress said, setting down a steaming cup of delicious liquid in front of him.

From the corner of his eye, he could see Holly shy away, doing the mental math in her head at the cost.

"The lady needs a hot chocolate," he told the waitress. "And we'll each have the special with soup." He looked over at Holly's wide eyes. "I'm paying."

Holly sat with her mouth hanging open.

"I'll be right back with that," the waitress replied, taking their menus.

"You don't have to do this," Holly stammered. "Really, it's not necessary."

"I'm paying for lunch," Nathan said firmly. "I suggested it. My treat."

"It's so much," she whispered, looking down at the table. "You really don't have to."

"I want to. Besides, I get a discount here."

She looked up at him, her face still saying she was unsure about accepting his offer. He could understand her hesitance. It was a lot of money to her, but hardly anything to him. She didn't know how much he made.

"Are you really sure? Because I'm impressed enough already. You don't have to spend two weeks' pay on lunch."

Nathan's eyes widened slightly. Two weeks' pay? Just how little money did she make? How was she skiing at Blue Aspen? She'd said she was a teacher, but he'd assumed she worked for a college or maybe as a private tutor.

A private tutor made sense. She would come with the family on a trip like this, but wouldn't have much money of her own.

"It's no problem," he assured her. "I can take it as a business expense. Please, let me buy lunch."

She sighed, chewing on the inside of her cheek for a moment. "Okay. I just don't want you to regret it later."

He chuckled. There was no way he would regret this

lunch. The only thing he would regret is that he didn't offer to pay for it in the first place. He found himself wanting to give Holly everything. It felt good to give her things.

"It's my pleasure," he told her. He pushed his untouched drink in front of her. "Here, try it."

She checked his face once more before hesitantly reaching for the drink. She checked in again with him before taking a sip.

"Oh, wow." She took a deeper sip, sighing with pleasure. "You weren't kidding. That's amazing."

Nathan grinned, leaning back in his chair. He liked seeing her smile and sigh like that. Her shoulders relaxed and she no longer looked like she might be sick. "I'm glad you like it."

"Thank you." Her green eyes met his and he felt a sizzle of desire sweep through him. Her smile warmed him. It made him wonder what she would look like in his bed. Would she blush just like she was now?

But a restaurant was not an appropriate place for a thought like that. Despite the storm, there were still a few other guests enjoying their lunches. Luckily, the waitress returned with a cup of hot chocolate for him. He sipped at it, trying to steer his thoughts away from the way her curves would feel under his fingers.

"Have you ever been to New York at Christmas time?" Nathan asked her. "You said you love Christmas. New York is famous for their Christmas spirit."

"I've actually never been to New York," she admitted. "I've seen a lot of the Midwest, Disneyland and Disney World, and I went to Mexico during college."

"Spring break?" He liked the idea of her in a bikini drinking to much tequila.

"An immersion class," she replied. "Although I did get some beach time. But, mostly I just walked around trying to get my verb tenses right."

"Do you speak Spanish?"

"Not as well as I'd like. I can sort of hold a conversation, but I'm working on it. Do you speak any other languages?"

"I'm trying to work on Mandarin," he said. "It's a tonal language, which makes it hard."

"What do you mean?" she asked, leaning in and looking interested.

"In English, you indicate that you're asking a question by raising your pitch at the end of the sentence," he explained.

"Like this?" She exaggerated the pitch change.

He nodded. "Exactly. In Chinese, that's part of the words themselves. It's not just the sounds, but the way the sounds are heard that's the language."

"Give me an example."

"If you say 'ma,' flat like in English, it means 'scold.' But, if you say 'ma?' Like you're looking for your mom, then that means 'rough.' But, if you say it up and down like you're whining, ma-a-a, that means horse. If you say it 'ma-a,' dropping pitch on the second part, it means mother."

"That sounds confusing," Holly said, shaking her head. "I would end up calling my mother a horse. A lot."

"You don't even want to know some of the things I've accidentally said." He chuckled. "I'm just glad my investors found it amusing that I tried. Luckily, the grammar is very easy."

"So how do you ask a question?" She smiled. "I ask, using the rising question tone. You wouldn't be able to use the upwards tone to ask, since that would mean a different word."

"You simply add the question sound to the end." He grinned at her. "It's ma."

"Oh great. Another ma."

She laughed and grinned at him, taking another sip of her hot chocolate. It was then that their food arrived.

"This looks amazing," she told him. She reached across the table and squeezed his hand. "Thank you."

"Want to hear more about Chinese?" he asked her.

"Definitely," she replied, picking up her fork. "Tell me everything you know."

CHAPTER 10

*M*erryweather

MERRYWEATHER FROWNED up at the mountain. Things were going well, but they needed more time.

Why couldn't things ever be simple?

Merryweather rubbed her hands together and thought of snow. She started to smile. Snow was the perfect answer for a winter love story.

Her sister would be so impressed. And probably a little envious, too.

The snow was just going to be so good.

CHAPTER 11

*H*olly

LUNCH WAS AMAZING. And not just because of the food.

While the food was delicious, it was the company that made it spectacular. Holly found herself laughing and smiling while she ate. She couldn't seem to stop smiling.

If this were a first date, she'd be inviting him up to her room for a drink.

"I'm really sorry to bother you," the waitress said, standing at their table. "But, we need to close. The snow's coming down too hard for us to stay open much longer."

Holly glanced outside through the huge window. White, fluffy flakes floated down and swirled around like the inside of a snow-globe. Already it looked like there was several inches of fresh powder.

"Of course," Nathan replied. He looked over at Holly. "You interested in doing a couple more runs? Or we could go to the hot-spring. I have a private pool reserved for the weekend."

"That sounds tempting." Holly bit her lower lip. A hot spring with Nathan? Nathan in a swimsuit? She wanted it.

"We could skip the skiing," Nathan offered. "What else are you doing tonight?"

"I actually have this party tonight." She glanced down at her watch, hoping that maybe she could fit in the hot-spring before her hair appointment.

In fact, way more time had passed than she thought. If she flew down the mountain, she might be able to make the appointment in time. She thought about canceling it, but she'd already paid. It was a lot of money.

"I'm actually late for my hair appointment," she groaned. She scrunched her face into an unhappy frown.

"Are you going to the Educator Award Fundraiser?" Nathan asked. They both stood from the table and went to retrieve their snow-gear.

"I am," Holly replied with a smile. "It's why I'm here this weekend."

Nathan nodded and looked like he'd just figured something out. She assumed it was why she was skiing at Blue Aspen and yet unable to afford lunch. She still felt a hint of embarrassment at not being able to pay for the meal as promised.

"Then go to your hair appointment. And I'll see you at the party."

"You're coming?" she asked, suddenly even more excited about it than before.

"I am," he replied with a smile. "And I expect the first dance with you."

"Done," she promised.

And maybe after we can go to the hot-spring, she thought to herself. The image of Nathan in a swimsuit beckoning her into a steaming pool was just too good of an idea to pass up.

They put on their winter gear and pushed open the wooden doors to go back outside. It took both of them pushing to get the door open. Snow had drifted against the door and the wind howled. Holly pulled her scarf up high around her nose.

Their skis had a couple of inches of snow sitting on them. Nathan laughed as they brushed them off, but Holly began to wonder if she would make it home tomorrow. This seemed like a lot of snow, even for the mountains.

The last run down the mountain was Holly's favorite. Thick snow coated the trails and she was able to swoosh and spray snow with every turn. With her fancy skis, she felt like a photographer should be following her.

But the bottom of the hill meant that she had to leave Nathan. Even though she knew she'd see him in just a couple of hours, she didn't want to be separated from him. The time they'd spent together today had been wonderful.

"You aren't going to ditch me tonight, are you?" she asked him as they skied into the basin and toward the ski rental return area. She clicked her skis from her boots and leaned them up against the side of the building.

"Not in a million years," he promised. He put a hand on his heart in promise. She felt a little better, but wished that it was already time for the fundraiser to start.

"Okay." She stood there awkwardly for a moment. She wanted to kiss him, but they both still had their helmets on and that had already failed once today. A hug? A handshake? A wave?

She went for the hug, wrapping her arms around him. Their bulky jackets got in the way, but it was still a decent hug. It was way better than a wave, at least.

"See you soon," he told her, giving her one last squeeze

before letting her go. "Do you need any help carrying these inside?"

"I got it," she replied, regretting it instantly. If he helped her, she could spend a couple more minutes with him.

"Nathan!" a deep male voice called out.

Holly turned to see a giant of a man heading toward them. He didn't have a jacket, but snow already covered his dark hair and the tops of his shoulders.

"Yes, Gregory?" Nathan turned and faced him.

"You have a phone call," the man informed him. Nathan sighed and looked at the man. The man grunted. Some more silent communication went on between them. Holly wasn't sure who Gregory was, but Nathan seemed to know him.

"Fine," Nathan said after a moment. "I'll be right up."

Gregory gave a curt nod and headed back to the hotel.

"Go answer your phone call," Holly told him when Nathan looked back to her. "I'll see you at the party."

A smile crossed his face. He stood before her and she wondered if he was going to attempt another kiss. She was willing to risk it if he was.

But then he simply smiled one last time and turned away. She hoisted her skis up on her shoulder and headed inside the rental building, giving one last glance at Nathan. His dark form disappeared into the heavy snow.

"THERE YOU ARE," Merryweather said as soon as Holly walked in. "I was afraid you were going to be late."

"For returning my gear?" Holly asked, handing the skis, poles, and helmet off to Merryweather.

"No for your hair appointment," Merryweather replied. "I'm managing a couple of stations today. The snow has us a little short-handed."

"Oh." Holly nodded as she sat down on a small wooden bench and took off her boots. She groaned with pleasure at the sensation of loosening the boots. They fit perfectly, but they were still ski boots and made to keep her ankles immobilized. It felt good to move them again.

"Come with me," Merryweather said, motioning Holly to just leave the boots on the floor. "I'll take you up."

Holly slid on her regular snow boots from the small storage area and followed Merryweather into the lobby. They went past the check-in desk and up a wide staircase. The hotel was quiet.

"What do you think of the snow?" Merryweather asked as they walked. "The weatherman is saying it's the storm of the century."

"It's that bad?" Holly looked over surprised.

"We've gotten nearly a foot and a half since lunch," Merryweather said, sounding almost proud. "And it doesn't show signs of stopping."

Holly paused, wondering just how she was going to get home tomorrow. The ski towns were all used to heavy snows, but this sounded like more snow than usual. She and Aliyah were supposed to leave tomorrow. What if the roads weren't clear?

"Don't you worry about the roads," Merryweather said, as if reading her mind. "The hotel has a policy for things like this. You'll stay in your room, free of charge until the roads are passable."

"Oh, that's good to know." Holly felt relief go through her. She wouldn't be stuck paying for a hotel room she couldn't afford because the snow was too deep for her ancient car.

"Here we go," Merryweather announced as they reached the salon. She pushed open the beautiful glass doors for Holly to walk through. "Oh, and this may seem odd, but do you have a dress for tonight?"

"My friend is letting me borrow one," Holly replied. It was an old bridesmaid dress, but it was formal and pretty enough that it didn't totally look like a bridesmaid dress. It had a designer label, which seemed important for tonight. "Why?"

"The hotel boutique got a couple of gowns in the mail yesterday. They didn't order any gowns, and the designer can't figure out where they came from. We're trying to find people to take them off our hands. I think one might be in your size."

"I can't afford a designer gown," Holly told her. "But thank you."

"Oh, I didn't explain that well. The boutique is giving the dresses away. The designer doesn't want to pay for return shipping and since the boutique didn't technically pay for them..." Merryweather glanced around like she was giving away a big secret. "It's a liability thing, apparently. Taxes or something."

"Well, I guess if it's free..." Holly shrugged.

Merryweather clapped her hands together gleefully. "Excellent! I'll have them brought up to the salon. You can try them on with your hair all done up."

"Okay. Thank you," Holly said. She couldn't believe her luck. Maybe the dresses wouldn't fit or be the right color, but it wouldn't hurt to try. They would probably be better than a hand-me-down bridesmaid dress.

The salon smelled of lavender and eucalyptus. Peaceful. Tranquil. Expensive.

Holly introduced herself to the front desk and they quickly whisked her away into the back. Holly sat in a traditional hair-salon chair in front of a giant floor to ceiling mirror. The front desk woman took Holly's ski-pants and jacket to hang and dry in the front. Holly felt a little silly sitting in the beautiful salon wearing long underwear and an old sweater.

"Hi Holly, I'm Flora." Her hairdresser stepped out from behind a doorway and greeted her. She had long hair the same color as Merryweather's and the most amazing blue eyes Holly had ever seen. They were so blue, they looked like they might be contact lenses.

She came over and ran her fingers over Holly's hair. "Up-do?" she asked, taking out the rubber band holding Holly's ponytail.

"Yes, please," she replied. "I just want it to look amazing. You're the stylist, so I'll go with your opinion."

Flora grinned. "I'll make you look like a princess. Do you mind if we listen to some Christmas music instead of the spa stuff?"

"Sure. I love Christmas music."

Flora flashed another grin at her before hitting a button on a big silver cart. The tranquil sounds of rain and Himalayan singing bowls disappeared, replaced with the sound of Alvin and the Chipmunks singing about hula-hoops.

"Oh shoot." Flora quickly pressed the button again. The music changed to a more tranquil rendition of "Silent Night." "It can still be peaceful music," she said.

Holly relaxed in the chair as Flora worked her magic. She had to be the best hairdresser Holly had ever had. Flora never pulled. She never snagged her comb in Holly's ear or sprayed water on her face. The hairspray didn't turn into a giant cloud around Holly's head, and the bobby-pins didn't pinch. If anything, Flora's fingers felt good on Holly's scalp.

"Do you mind if I text my friend?" Holly asked Flora.

"Of course not," Flora replied. "Just as long as you hold still."

Holly carefully pulled her phone from her pocket and texted Aliyah.

> *Hey. How are you feeling? You coming to the party tonight?*

HARDLY ANY TIME passed before her phone chirped with a new message.

> *Better, but I think I'm staying in. My stomach still feels like it might explode if I move to fast, so dancing is a bad idea. You okay by yourself?*

HOLLY GRINNED. She was doing way better than just okay.

> *Yeah. Remind me to tell you about the guy I met. You'd be proud of me.*

ALIYAH TEXTED her back a thumbs up as well as an eggplant emoji. Holly rolled her eyes and put her phone away. She wished Aliyah was feeling up for the party, but was glad she was at least doing better. That sandwich really knocked her for a loop.

"Who is doing your makeup?" Flora asked, pinning a curl to the side of Holly's head.

"I was just going to do it myself," Holly admitted. "My friend Aliyah said she would help."

"I don't mean to be pushy, but I'd love to do it for you," Flora said. The curling iron clicked and hissed as she put it in Holly's hair. "I wouldn't charge you. I'm taking a class and I'd love the practice. Your bone structure would be so much fun to work with."

"Um, sure?" Holly shrugged.

"And don't worry, I plan on a more natural look. But, I think a little bit of smoky eye mixed with a good eyeliner, maybe some red lipstick...well that depends on your dress..." Flora started rambling on, coming up with her plan.

Holly let her ramble. She was having fun. She could see the shape of the up-do Flora was creating and couldn't wait to see the end result. Her dirty-blonde hair looked shiny and perfect. It almost didn't look like her real hair, it was so lovely.

"Here's the dresses," Merryweather announced, stepping into the salon area and holding up two garment bags. "One's blue and the other is pink."

"I like the idea of a pink one," Flora said, giving one last spray of hairspray. "Is it still snowing out there?"

"Like crazy," Merryweather replied. She almost sounded proud of the snow outside. "The locals all say they've never seen anything like it."

"I hope it doesn't go too overboard," Flora replied, pursing her lips at Merryweather. "We can't stay here forever."

"Oh, I know." Merryweather hung the dresses and pulled open the bags. "Oh, it's not blue. It's actually green."

Flora leaned over from where she was standing and smiled. "I think the green one is actually going to be the winner. Let's see her try them on."

Holly stood up and looked at the two dresses. The pink

one looked soft and feminine. The pink was pretty without being too girlish. The cut was mermaid with a lace overlay that took away much of the pink color and softened it.

The green dress caught her eye though. It was a dark emerald with a deep v-neck and beautiful silver bead work. It reminded Holly of the 1920's, but in a modern design. It was elegant, yet sexy.

She could see herself wearing it and dancing with Nathan.

"I'll try the pink one first," she said, standing up and taking the dress. Flora directed her to a small room off to the side where she could change. She quickly put on the pink dress and stepped out.

Both Flora and Merryweather frowned. So did Holly when she looked in the mirror.

"It's not bad," Flora told her. "It's just not... you."

Holly hurried back and put on the green dress. It felt soft on her skin and she loved the weight of the beading.

"Oh my," Merryweather gasped when Holly stepped out.

"Oh my, indeed," Flora agreed. "That's the dress."

Holly looked in the mirror and thought a princess was looking back at her. She looked radiant. Lovely. Slim and yet curvy at the same time. The green of the dress brought out the green of her eyes.

"Let's finish that makeup," Flora said, motioning Holly in the mirror to come back and sit down. "It's almost time for the party."

CHAPTER 12

*M*erryweather

THEY WERE perfect for one another. Merryweather could see the strands of love starting to bind them together. The magic of love mixed with the magic of Christmas, making a heady combo for Merryweather to work with.

She rubbed her hands together once again, excited at the possibilities before her.

Love like this didn't happen every day. This was where magic came from.

CHAPTER 13

$\mathcal{H}$olly

"Hot damn, girl!" Aliyah whistled when Holly walked into the bedroom of their suite to grab her shoes. "Where did you get that dress?"

"It was from the hotel. Kind of a fluke thing," Holly replied. "You like it?"

"Like it? I love it. It's perfect. It's like it was made for you," Aliyah told her. "You look like a freaking princess."

Holly looked over at her friend, taking her in. Aliyah was still in bed, a big silver bowl in the bed with her. There were saltines and ginger ale on the nightstand.

"You doing okay?" Holly asked, feeling guilt creep in at leaving her friend.

"I'm doing great," Aliyah assured her. "Well, other than my stomach deciding that it doesn't need to keep anything down. I've gotten through nearly half a season of *Game of Thrones*."

"I don't want any spoilers," Holly reminded her. She went to the window and peeked out. Snow was still coming down hard. The entire ski basin was covered in a thick blanket of fresh powder.

"I'll try not to," Aliyah promised. "Is it still snowing? I heard they might let us stay an extra day if we can't get out."

"Are you okay with that?" Holly asked, closing the curtain and turning back to Aliyah.

"Heck yeah. I don't want to teach like this." She motioned to the silver bowl and ginger ale. "Besides, I still have half a season to watch. I already called the school and gave them a warning. They said it'll probably be a snow day there, too. It's super lucky."

Luck seemed to be on Holly's side this weekend. She chuckled and slid on her black heels. They weren't super fancy, but they were comfortable. No one would see them anyway since they would be under the hem of the dress.

"Have a blast," Aliyah told her, pulling the covers up to her chin. "I want to hear all about it. And your day. You said it was good?"

"Great." Holly felt a warmth fill her core. "I met this guy. His name's Nathan."

"Ooo," Aliyah sat up a little in bed. "Tell me more."

I couldn't stop the smile from creeping across my face as I thought about him. "Well, he likes to read, he's funny, and he can't throw a snowball to save his life."

Aliyah laughed. "Is he cute?"

"Super cute. He's got short dark brown hair, and these amazing dark eyes. Like, movie-star eyes. And his smile is just a little bit crooked, but in a way that makes his whole face light up when he smiles. Plus, he's got these... You're laughing at me."

Aliyah sat snickering in the bed. "I'm sorry." She put her hands to her mouth. "It's just that you're gushing. You look so damn happy. If I didn't know better, I'd say you're in love."

"Love?" I scoffed. "I just met the guy. We haven't even spent a full day together yet."

"Maybe you found the one. Maybe it's a Christmas miracle," Aliyah teased. "I'm just glad that you are having fun. It's nice to see you happy again. I haven't seen you smile like that in months."

"I feel happy," Holly admitted. "Maybe it's just getting away from all the negative talk in town. Maybe it's being on vacation. Maybe it's Nathan."

"My money's on Nathan," Aliyah told her. "You should see the smile on your face when you say his name."

Holly blushed. And thought about Nathan and smiled.

"Get out of here," Aliyah told her. "I have dragons to watch. You have men to seduce and smile at." She gave Holly a wink.

Holly shook her head and picked up her purse. She checked her makeup in the mirror by the door. It was still perfect. Flora was amazing. He looked up and down at the green dress, the curled and styled hair, and the eyelashes that went on for days.

She gave herself a thumbs up and headed down to the party.

THE HOTEL HAD a beautiful reception area located to the the west of the lobby. The walls matched the rustic wood-cabin look of the hotel, but the inside was elegant and ornate. The center of the room had a dozen beautifully decorated tables, all with centerpieces of evergreen and flickering candles. Crystal chandeliers hung from the ceiling, huge windows overlooked the snowy mountains outside, and beautiful people mingled drinking champagne. There was a fireplace and several cozy looking nooks with comfortable leather chairs along the back walls. A giant Christmas tree stood by one of the windows. The sparkling lights in the tree reflected on the dark windows like winter fireflies.

A man at the door took her ticket and gave her directions on how to find her table for dinner. She didn't really need them. The table for the VIPs sat in the center of the room in full view of the other tables, and she could see the placard with her name on it from the entrance.

She was the "guest of honor" for tonight. It was framed as an awards ceremony, but it was more of a fundraiser. There were supposed to be lots of rich and famous people here tonight, all donating money to education initiatives. She was just the face of their work for the evening.

Holly picked up a glass of champagne from one of the servers and made her way to the table. There was to be dinner and speeches, and then a reception to follow. There was an open bar and she'd ordered the prime-rib for dinner, although she now felt it would be too much after lunch.

Still, she was excited.

"There you are," Merryweather greeted her. "Come have a seat. We're about to begin." The woman now wore a dark blue business suit and had her silver hair pulled into a tight bun. Holly still couldn't place her age. She was simultaneously twenty-six and seventy-three.

"Thank you," Holly said as Merryweather walked her to the table. "Do you just do all the jobs around here?"

Merryweather laughed. "This snow has a lot of the staff home-bound. I live within walking distance, so I'm happy to come in so they can stay safe with their families. Besides, I love a good party."

Merryweather pulled out a heavy wooden chair at the head table for Holly to sit in. Most of the other chairs were filled, except for the one in the middle. Holly couldn't see the name placard, but whomever it was, obviously was the main host for the night. It was probably someone from one of the sponsoring companies.

Holly sipped on her champagne and watched as guests arrived. The ballroom seemed slightly empty, but she assumed it was probably due to the snow. Slowly people began to take their seats as servers notified everyone that the food would be arriving shortly.

That's when Holly saw Nathan. She nearly dropped her glass of champagne.

He wore a stunning black tuxedo. He'd shaved and smoothed his dark hair back. He looked like something out of a movie. He was more suave than James Bond. More handsome than Prince Charming. Sexier than Christian Grey.

He paused at the edge of the tables, his brown eyes scanning the faces. A slight frown creased his brow as he looked. Merryweather tugged at his elbow, pointing to the edge of the room. Holly thought of calling to him, or at least waving, but this was a fancy party. Merryweather pulled him to the side of the room.

The lights dimmed, and Holly realized that there was a projection screen to her right. The words "**Educators make the world bright**" flashed across the screen. A video montage of stock-photo children with teachers in perfect classrooms scrolled across the screen. Luckily, they shifted into the various real teachers who had been nominated for the award and the images became less forced. Holly sipped on her champagne, and then nearly spit it out when her smiling face filled the screen.

Small clips of her laughing with her students danced across the screen. She heard herself saying words about education and the importance of treating children with respect and finding what made kids want to learn. She remembered giving an interview on camera upon winning the award.

She grimaced as she listened to herself. Her voice sounded too high and she wished she had said something more profound. She glanced around the room, but luckily all the guests seemed to be smiling at the screen and nodding their heads. Maybe she didn't sound as dumb as she was afraid of being.

The lights rose and the room filled with applause. Holly felt her cheeks heat. She knew she'd won the Educator of the Year award, but she still wasn't prepared for the public video or the fact that everyone was now staring at her.

Everyone, including Nathan. He stood at the edge of the tables, a microphone in one hand and the award trophy in the other. Their eyes met and he grinned at her.

"Thank you all for coming," he said into the microphone, his eyes still on Holly. The room stilled and turned to look at him.

"My name is Nathan Reed. I'm the CEO of Paradigm Technologies and will be presenting the award to this year's Educator of the Year award." He paused, giving a small smile to Holly.

Her stomach tightened and went ice cold while her cheeks turned to fire.

Nathan was the CEO of Paradigm Technologies? This was the man buying out her town's company. This was the man who was ruining the lives of everyone she cared about.

And yet, she didn't hate him. Not when he smiled at her like that.

Her mind began to race. *Maybe he doesn't know about Elements Computers' move to California,* she thought to herself. *Maybe it's one of his underlings. Maybe this is fate's way of fixing things. Maybe this is the Christmas miracle Devonsville needs.*

"I was lucky enough to meet Ms. Jones earlier today," Nathan continued. "I can see why her students adore her. She's smart and funny, and a pro at dodge-ball. She'll make you feel like the most important person in the world with just a smile."

The crowd chuckled and Nathan made his way toward the main table. Holly couldn't tear her eyes away from him. Every step closer made her heart pound just a little bit harder.

"This year, I am honored and proud to give Ms. Holly Jones the Educator of the Year award." He now stood next to her. The spotlight centered on the two of them as she rose to her feet and he handed her the trophy. He shook her hand, posing for a photographer. Applause filled the room.

Holly hoped the picture came out okay. She only knew she was smiling because her cheeks hurt. Otherwise, her entire body was numb with shock.

And then Nathan handed her the microphone.

She fumbled with the award and the microphone, nearly dropping both but managing to keep them both in her hands.

"Wow." She glanced around the room. Nathan had made it look so easy talking to all these fancy people. She was used to speaking in front of children, not adults. "First of all, thank you. I know that students nominate a teacher for this award, so I need to thank my class."

Applause caught her off guard.

"My students and the families that raise them are the most important things in my world," she continued. "I thank you for this award."

She'd had a much longer and far more eloquent speech prepared, but upon seeing Nathan, it all went completely out of her head. She sat down hard in her chair and took a big gulp of champagne. The applause for her speech continued for a moment and then died down.

"Please enjoy the rest of your dinner," Nathan said, taking the microphone. "Remember there's an open bar and we are still taking donations for the literacy campaign. Thank you all and have a wonderful time tonight."

The lights went back up and Holly felt the spotlight leave her like a physical release. She took another sip of champagne and looked over to see Nathan sitting in the chair next to her and grinning.

"So you really are a teacher," he said, and then began to laugh.

CHAPTER 14

*N*athan

WHEN HOLLY SAID she was a teacher, he'd assumed private tutor or possibly college professor. He didn't expect her to actually be a public school teacher, let alone the one he was giving an award to. He hadn't paid any attention to the name of the recipient for tonight's award. He never did. He learned it two seconds before the speech and promptly forgot it once the applause came.

He wouldn't be forgetting the name this time.

He took his seat next to her, sipping on champagne and excited about the evening. This award just became a lot more fun.

"So you're Nathan Reed?" she asked him. Her green eyes held a touch of concern, as if she were no longer certain of him.

"The one and only," he replied.

She looked like she was about to say something, but their

food arrived. He was still full from lunch, so he didn't plan on eating much. He looked over to see Holly had her fork and knife ready, but pausing at the plate.

She set her fork down and turned to face him. Her brow was serious and her mouth set in a thin line.

"Do you know anything about Elements Computer Technologies?"

Nathan thought for a moment, trying to place the name. Lucy had mentioned it. "I believe my company just acquired it," he replied. "We just acquired three companies with the finalizations coming at the end of the year. It's been a crazy couple of months."

He didn't want to think about RentTech tonight. The name sounded familiar, but since he'd been preoccupied with RentTech, he wasn't sure. Lucy would know. She'd managed things for him. He wasn't sure what all she'd done, but he was sure it would make money for them both.

"Oh." Holly looked disappointed. "Do you know anything about them moving the headquarters?"

He thought he remembered Lucy telling him something about a tax deal. He'd been so focused on RentTech that he wasn't sure what was going on. "Not really. I'm trying to take this weekend off from work."

She nodded, her brow still dark. She opened her mouth to say something, then shut it, then open it again. "Elements Computer Technologies' headquarters is in my hometown."

He wasn't quite sure what the connection was.

"The move is taking the major employer from my town." Her words started slowly, but came out quicker and more emotional as she spoke. "If you could do something about it or even stop it, it would save our town. I know that we just met, but..."

He smiled at her. "I promise that I'll look into it."

The crease between Holly's eyebrows smoothed. "Really? Just like that?"

"I can't promise anything, but I will look into it," he told her. "I'm happy to help. I want to help."

She nodded. "The work contracts all start ending at the end of the year, so there's still a little time. Thank you. Thank you so much."

She reached out, taking his hand and squeezing it. Her touch sent heat straight into his groin and made his head swim like he'd had too much wine. Something primal and wonderful filled him. If this was his response to a simple touch on the hand, Nathan smiled as he wondered what would happen if he kissed her. And what would happen after that.

She grinned at him, looking like an unexpected weight had lifted from her shoulders. He hoped he wouldn't disappoint her. He still needed to look over the plans on how to integrate ECT into Paradigm Technologies. He knew that Lucy was interested in making the most money as quickly as possible. It was why she made such an excellent right hand man, so to speak.

"So, tell me more about being a teacher," he said to Holly, changing the subject. "How much did you bribe the kids to nominate you? Cookies? Gold star stickers? An extra minute at recess?"

Holly laughed at his joking tone. "I actually didn't know I was even nominated until the phone call came," she admitted. "I had heard of the award, but I'm just doing what I know how to do. I'm not that exceptional."

Nathan had to disagree about that. Everything about this beautiful woman was exceptional.

"I'm actually really glad I won," she said, looking down and then up at him through her long lashes. "I got to come here and meet you."

Nathan had heard his share of pickup lines in his life. As a billionaire, there were always trophy-wife-want-to-bes and women looking for an easy life. Some went the route of looking sexy. Others used their intelligence.

This didn't feel like he was being used. This was a compliment. It was honest and heartfelt. Corny, yes, but wonderful at the same time. The slight pink in her cheeks as she said it made it all the better.

He held up his champagne glass. "Cheers to that."

She grinned, tapping her glass against his. They both sipped at the champagne and smiled.

Nathan wanted to ask her more about her classroom and her students, but it was time for another speech. He wasn't giving this one, but it would be rude to whisper and giggle with Holly while someone presented another award and explained more about where donations went to help children and educators succeed.

Dinner continued, filled with speeches that interrupted his conversations with Holly. He never did like these speeches, and now they dragged on into eternity. The thing that made it bearable and torture at the same time was the fact that Holly sat next to him.

Finally, the dinner and eternal speeches ended. It was now time for the reception. Even before Nathan had met Holly, this was the part of the evening that made the speeches worthwhile. This was where the party happened.

Everyone stood from their chairs and scattered into the comfortable room. Live music started to play. The bar made more drinks. There were several casino-type tables set up for guests to play with pretend money. Dealers for blackjack, roulette, craps, and even poker filed into the room and stood ready to entice the players.

The chips would be fake, but the buy-ins were real. All

the money went to the charity and the donors left with fabulous prizes and a tax-write off for their business.

Meanwhile, hotel staff cleared the dinner tables, replacing them with smaller cocktail areas and comfortable seating. The lights dimmed and candles were lit. The sounds of merrymaking and Christmas songs filled the room.

"This is amazing," Holly whispered, watching as Merryweather directed several employees on where to put the tables. The room magically transformed from a dining area into a comfortable lounge in a matter of moments.

"You having fun?" he asked her.

She nodded. "But I do need another drink."

"Let me buy you a drink," he replied, offering his arm and guiding her toward the bar. His heart skipped a beat at her giggle and the way she wrapped her arm around his. It wasn't often that a woman had this effect on him. In fact, it had been a long time since he'd felt this level of excitement toward a woman at merely the touch of her hand.

She ordered more champagne and wandered around the room. He didn't want to go to the casino tables. Most of the guests had headed in that direction, crowding the tables and shouting with pleasure when they won or lost.

It would be difficult to carry on a conversation there, and that's what he found himself wanting to do with Holly.

"Nathan. Wonderful speech."

Nathan turned to see a friend of his, coming to greet him.

"Graham? What are you doing here?" Nathan asked, giving the man in a tux a warm hug. Graham was slightly shorter than Nathan with lighter hair and eyes. As they were of a similar age, they'd found themselves friends.

"My secretary said I have to start doing more positive PR," Graham replied, rolling his eyes. "Apparently, just launching rockets isn't enough anymore."

Nathan chuckled. "Graham, I'd like to introduce you to

Holly Jones. She earned this years' award. Holly, this is my friend Graham."

Graham held out his hand and shook Holly's with a firm grip. "It's a pleasure to meet you. What grade did you say you teach?"

"Second grade," Holly replied.

"What age is that?" Graham asked her.

"Seven to eight years old," Holly answered. "It's an amazing age."

"I'm glad you think so," Graham told her, shaking his head. "I'm afraid they would eat me alive."

Holly looked surprised. "But you're Graham Bell. All of my students adore you. I had three write that you are their favorite inventor this year."

"Are you sure they didn't mean Alexander Graham Bell?" Graham teased, making Holly laugh.

The fact that another man had her laughing made Nathan's mouth go sour. Graham was a handsome and single man. Holly had known who he was. Granted, most of the world could recognize the billionaire who now specialized in rockets and space technology. Still, he didn't like the awe in the way she looked at him. Jealousy tried to rear its ugly head.

"I'm afraid I'm not any good with kids," Graham continued. The polite but nonplussed blink was quick across Holly's face. "I don't like them and they don't like me."

"I'm sorry to hear that," she told him, her voice losing the laughter. The jealousy disappeared. Holly wouldn't want anyone who didn't like children. They were her world. Graham wasn't his competition. At least, not in this.

"Would you please excuse me?" Graham asked. "I see the a seat at the poker table just opened up and I'm feeling lucky. My friend Alex is there and I need to steal his money."

Nathan recognized the man at the craps table as another

billionaire. A lovely young woman was laughing at something witty he'd just said.

"Good luck," Holly said, giving Graham a smile. It grated on Nathan's nerves that she even did that for him.

"Thank you." Graham grinned back at her before turning to Nathan. "Would you care to join me?"

"Not tonight," Nathan replied. He took a step closer to Holly.

"I think you've already won the grand prize tonight," Graham said softly, shaking Nathan's hand before going to the tables.

Holly stared after him. "Wow. Two billionaires. I met two billionaires today. No one is going to believe me."

Nathan chuckled. "And you haven't even seen the entire guest list," he told her.

"What, is there a trillionaire that's coming as well?" She winked at him. "Or maybe some famous actor or band?"

"You don't recognize the band now?" Nathan asked, motioning to the stage where musicians sang holiday songs.

Holly frowned, taking a step toward the music. Then her eyes went wide. "Is that really the Tones?"

"When you have three billionaires in attendance, you tend to get good music," Nathan told her. He enjoyed watching her reaction as she realized it was the famous rock group. Later, they would play their own music.

They continued to walk around the room, making their way to the windows where it was slightly quieter and more intimate.

"Is this how your normal life works?" Holly asked him. "Famous rich people, rock stars and money?"

Nathan shrugged. "It's not usually this crowded."

She shook her head. They found a little love seat nestled into the window overlooking the ski basin. Snow still came down hard and fast. Night had come and now the flakes danced under the lights of the ski-resort.

Her leg rested next to his. The chair was too small for them to truly sit apart, and Nathan found his heart beating faster just being near her. This felt intimate, despite the fact that there were other people just on the other side of the room.

"Oh look," Holly said, pointing upward. "Mistletoe."

Nathan's eyes went up and saw that someone had hung a small sprig of green over the love seat. Given that it was a love seat, he could understand the placement.

"You said you don't really like holiday things," Holly said, her eyes still on the greenery. "How do you feel about mistletoe?"

"I think I can learn to like it," he replied.

And then he kissed her.

$\mathcal{H}$olly

THE KISS STARTED slow and sweet. It was just his lips pressed against hers, but then his fingers came to her face and she wanted more.

A lot more.

Her hand went to his neck, pulling him into her. Her fingertips played with the bottom of his hair. He pulled back, her eyes still closed. He smelled of a masculine soap that made her breathe him in as deep as she could.

The crowd disappeared from her mind. The band's music faded, and the laughter receded until all she heard was the sound of her own heartbeat and Nathan's soft breathing.

Slowly, she opened her eyes, looking up and into his handsome face. His cheeks were flushed as if he'd been running in the cold. She could feel his breathing come hard and fast. His eyes were dark, pupils wide and not just because of the dim candlelight.

Apparently he wasn't the only one experiencing the flush of a mistletoe kiss.

She kissed him this time. Pulling her into him and wrapping her arm around his neck. There was no stubble against her cheeks. Her tongue found his and a shiver of pure desire shot straight through her.

She pulled back this time, their foreheads pressed together as they both gasped for air. The electric intensity between them had her vibrating with need. She remembered the room full of people. The sound of music slowly came back to her.

"You want to get out of here?" he asked. His hand still rested on the back of her neck, the other on her hip. His gaze dropped to her mouth and he unconsciously licked his lips.

"Yeah." It was all the English she could manage. Even then, it came out more as a grunt than a word.

His lips turned into a smug smile. He stood, holding out a hand for her to join him. She loved the way her hand folded into his, like it was meant to be there. It felt like magic when he touched her. She grinned as they crossed the room, oblivious to the party and the drinks.

She didn't even notice that the band was playing her favorite Christmas carol. She didn't notice the man at the roulette table hit a red seven for all his chips. She didn't see the three tables hit blackjack at the same time. She didn't notice the royal flush at the poker table.

All she saw was Nathan and all she knew was that she was the luckiest girl in the world.

Merryweather nodded to them, a knowing look in her pale lavender eyes. She gave Holly a wink and a smile before continuing back to the event.

NATHAN GUIDED her through the hallways of the hotel. She giggled, holding the hem of her dress as they ran through the empty corridors, slowing only when they hit the lobby. There they managed to walk sedately.

But, even then, they were grinning like idiots. Holly felt like a teenager, giddy with her first boyfriend. Only this was better than prom, this was better than the cheap Motel 6 and judging from the build of Nathan's shoulders, this was going to be a lot better than the six point three seconds her prom date had given her.

"Did you know there are two men following us?" Holly whispered, motioning her head to the two men pretending not to follow them. They looked out of place wearing their ski-attire while everyone else in the building wore tuxedos.

Nathan glanced back and chuckled. "They're mine. Don't worry about them."

Her eyebrows raised. Nathan had bodyguards. This was definitely different than what she was used to.

They made it to the elevator without attracting too much attention. They stood politely, a respectable distance apart as Nathan hit the button for the top floor. The smooth silver doors slid shut.

And then Nathan had her pinned to the wall, his body trapping her as his mouth found hers. She whimpered, arching her back and wishing that the elevator would go faster and slower at the same time. The faster they got to his room, the better, but she didn't want this kiss to end either.

The elevator chimed their arrival and reluctantly Nathan pulled back. His eyes were dark with desire and his hair mussed from her hands. She didn't remember putting her fingers in his hair, yet she wasn't surprised either. He stole her senses with his kisses.

She couldn't wait to see what he did with more than just a kiss.

Nathan slid his key-card into the slot at the door, and stepped inside. Holly hesitated for a nanosecond. She usually waited until there were multiple dates. She wasn't impulsive. She never slept with a man on the first date, let alone the first day of knowing him.

Yet, she couldn't deny this attraction. Even before she knew he was a billionaire, he was everything she wanted in a man. He was smart and funny. He made her laugh and at the same time made her insides heat with desire.

The sexual attraction was more powerful than anything she'd experienced. The kiss had been in the top three of her entire life, and just the thought of having more than kisses made her damp with excitement.

It didn't matter that he was Nathan Reed. He had already endeared himself to her before she knew who he was or what he could do for her and the town. To her, he was Prince Charming, and who said no to Prince Charming?

So she decided to take the risk. To let the magic of the day carry her into what could happen next. She let her body do the thinking for once, rather than her head. This wasn't about the town. This was about her and the fact that she wanted him. He could have been the busboy having a day on the slopes, and she still would have felt this way about him.

She went into the hotel room and gasped.

She might have still felt the same way about him if he were a busboy, but they certainly wouldn't have a room like this if he were.

Floor-to-ceiling windows lined a room bigger than her apartment. The snow came down fiercely over the dark mountains, but the room was comfortably warm. A fire already roared in a two-way fireplace and she could see just the hint of a king-sized bed on the opposite side. Everything was comfortable and elegant, just like the rest of the hotel.

She let her dress hem fall from her hand as she took in

the room. For once, she didn't feel under-dressed in this place. She and the dress fit in this room.

Nathan took off his black tuxedo jacket, tossing it casually onto a dining room chair. He tugged at his bow-tie, carelessly throwing it to rest with the jacket.

His white dress shirt fit like a dream. She'd only really seen him in his ski clothes, and they had hid the strength of his shoulders and the wonderful tapering of his waist. He was built. The man worked out. Holly swallowed hard, her hand playing with the heavy fabric of her skirt.

"Drink?" he offered, motioning to the bar to her left.

Holly shook her head, crossing the room. She put both her hands on either side of his face and kissed him. He groaned his approval, wrapping his arms around her and pulling him to her.

The intense and sudden jolt of desire caught her breath. Every fiber in her being said she was doing the right thing. There was lust and desire, yet something else too. Something deeper and sweeter than just the physical.

She didn't stop to think about or analyze the feeling. She just let her body take control. She let her brain stop worrying and fretting. She let herself have fun.

Her hand went to his shirt, nimbly unbuttoning the shiny white buttons. She was surprised to see that she wasn't shaking, even though her whole body was vibrating with desire. She tugged at his shirt and he shrugged out of it, barely breaking the kiss in the process.

Then, with a smooth motion, he lifted the hem of his undershirt up and over his head, giving her bare skin. She whimpered, her hands splaying against the strong muscles of his chest and abs. There was just enough hair to make him masculine, but not so much to make her think of a beast. The heat of his body through her fingers drove her wild.

She felt his hand on the back of her dress as he fumbled

for the zipper. She held still for him as he pulled downward, the zipper sliding free with a soft hiss. The dress crumpled to the floor in a beautiful heap of satin and beading.

His fingers caressed the curves of her shoulders, rounding across the tops of her breasts and then splaying on the curve of her hips. His fingers explored her skin, touching and making her shiver with want.

She reached behind her and unclasped her bra. It took a little doing, but she got it off without too much effort, tossing it to the ground. She was rewarded with a tight inhale from Nathan, his pupils blowing as he stared in wonder. He licked his lips.

He cupped her breasts with his hands, being careful of the delicate flesh. She sucked in an inhale and arched her back, groaning as his fingers brushed her nipples. Her nipples pebbled under his touch, sending lightning bolts of lust straight to her groin.

He dipped his head, putting his mouth to her chest. Her breathing became ragged as he caressed her nipple with his tongue and then gently took it between his teeth.

"So beautiful," he whispered against her skin. His finger drew the curve of her breast into her rib-cage. "So, so, beautiful."

She grinned at him. "Take me to bed," she told him.

His dark eyes flashed with lust and he grabbed her hand. They practically sprinted across the living room, past the fireplace, and into the luxurious bedroom. The lights were low and the firelight cast flickering shadows across the bed.

She bit her lip and reached for his belt. He helped her, able to undo the belt and buttons faster than she could. He kicked free of his pants and hooked his socks with his fingers, tossing them to the floor. Then he slipped free of his briefs, leaving him gloriously naked.

She stared for a moment, amazed by his body.

He was perfect. Strong and lean but not overly so. He didn't look fake or like he spent every moment of the day in the gym with steroids. He looked real. Strong.

And totally ready to go.

He hooked his fingers into the tiny fabric triangle at the apex of her legs. With a confident smile, he tugged downward and suddenly she was naked.

"I was right," he whispered, a smug grin on his face.

"What?" she asked.

"Still absolutely beautiful," he told her.

She grinned at the compliment. "Do you have a condom?"

He walked to his suitcase on the side of the room and knelt, searching the front pouch. She took the opportunity to admire the curve of his ass and the muscles of his leg.

Nathan did not skip leg day.

He held one up triumphantly, slid it on, and then walked back to her. She liked the way he looked, excited and ready to go.

He kissed her as they tumbled together onto the mattress. The soft, poofy comforter cradled their bodies as they landed. Her legs wrapped around his, wanting to join with him.

His hand went to her belly, then slid south. She groaned as he pressed his fingers against her. He swirled his fingers, listening as her breath caught and finding just the right places to touch. Muscles tightened and her legs spread, giving him access to more of her.

He slid one finger first, testing the waters. She heard a groan and saw him bite his lower lip as he slid in a second finger. His thumb stayed out, strumming her like a guitar as his fingers explored.

"So tight," he whispered, working magic with his entire hand.

Her brain fuzzed with hot lust. Her eyes fluttered and

heat coursed up and down her spine with every thrust of his fingers. She wanted so much more, but she didn't dare ask him to stop. Not when it felt this good.

Her muscles tightened and her eyes rolled into the back of her head. She was surprised at how quickly she found her climax. Nathan made it easy. There was almost no effort needed because he turned her on that much. His touch, his scent, and the sexy sound of his excited breathing put her over the edge and into pure bliss.

She lay gasping, her legs twitching with the intensity of pleasure he'd managed to find so quickly.

"More?" Nathan asked, his smile smug and proud of what he'd just accomplished.

She pointed to his very impressive erection. "More," she agreed.

He angled over her, his strong arms holding him above her. She looked up and into his brown eyes, seeing galaxies in them.

Slowly, so slowly that time seemed to hold its breath, he pressed into her. Completing her.

The first thrust was ecstasy. The second, heaven. She almost hated that he had to pull back in order to thrust again because it felt so damn good to have him inside of her.

She loved the way he groaned, the ragged way his breath caught as he filled her. There was a reverence, as if every motion of being with her was a little piece of heaven for him as well. Her hands went to his muscled back, reaching to pull him further inside of her. It felt like she could never get enough, even though she was full to bursting.

He kept a slow and steady pace, taking his time and exploring her. He dipped his head, his mouth finding her breast again, his hands exploring her curves as he worked his hips. Together, slowly, they worked towards climax.

It wasn't a sprint. It was a slow burn that slowly turned

into a raging inferno. She'd never wanted someone this badly in her life. She needed him to explode into her. It was the only way to put out the fire raging inside. The fire that he had built.

Holly opened her eyes and found herself looking into heaven. Nathan stared down at her, sweat on his brow and desire in his eyes. He looked at her like she was the most beautiful thing he had ever seen. He looked at her like she was magical.

It was enough to send them both spiraling into beautiful oblivion together. Holly wasn't sure who came first. It didn't matter. They came together, their bodies finally finding the release they both desperately needed. He claimed her. It was primal and powerful, but she claimed him as well in that moment.

Time stopped and ceased to matter. Nathan was the only real thing in her world.

They shattered and reformed around one another. This was something special. It was more than just a shared sensation. It was a shared connection. Their eyes held, finding that they shared the same heartbeat.

This was magic.

*N*athan

NATHAN WOKE to the soft sound of snoring.

He opened one eye, and found the most beautiful woman in the world sleeping next to him. Her head had fallen off the pillow, but her arm was draped across his chest. He smiled, watching her sleep for a moment.

He still couldn't believe this was real. The connection. The way she made him feel. It was like fireworks going off inside of him the moment he touched her. He felt like a sixteen-year-old boy, unable to contain his unending enthusiasm for her. Luckily, he managed to perform better than a sixteen-year-old boy.

Not to mention, he'd felt this attraction before she knew who he was. That almost kiss after the snowball fight told him that she'd wanted him even then. For the first time in a long time, he felt confident that she wasn't just interested in him for his money.

She actually liked him. That alone made her precious to him.

She murmured in her sleep, moving closer to him. The sheet fell from her chest, exposing one perfect breast in the pale morning light. He stared at it. She was better than a work of art. Her lines and curves were worthy of famous painters, and yet he was the one able to touch them. He wished he could paint, if only to capture her beauty for a moment in time.

He lay there, struggling with a dilemma. If he woke her, they could have sex again. If he let her sleep, he could continue to watch and admire her. Both options were fantastic.

He decided to let her sleep. When she woke, he could have the second option then. He could be patient, even if it was growing increasingly hard to do so.

Her eyelids fluttered and she took a deep breath. One green eye peeked open and a slow smile filled her face. She ran her hand across his chest, smiling wider as she did so.

"I thought I might have dreamed you," she said, her voice rough with sleep. The rasp was sexy as hell and his body instantly responded.

"I hope it was a good dream," he replied, reaching over and stroking a stray strand of hair from her cheek. She hummed with pleasure as she leaned into his hand.

"Very," she told him. And then she froze. Her eyes went wide and she sat straight up. "What time is it?"

"Does it matter?" he asked with a shrug.

"Check out is at ten-thirty." She threw off the covers and then stared down at her naked body for a moment. "And I have work tomorrow."

She picked up her phone, unlocking it and then sighing.

"It's only nine." She flopped back into bed, now scrolling

through her messages. Her smile grew bigger. "And we're snowbound. There is no checkout today."

"Snowbound?" Nathan repeated.

She nodded and jumped out of bed, full of energy. He liked that. He liked that energy and hoped she'd bring it back into the bed with her. Instead, she threw open the curtains, nearly blinding both of them with the sudden influx of brightness.

The world was solid white outside. The lifts weren't running and even the edges of the windows were frosted with snow.

"Aliyah messaged me," Holly explained. "We got so much snow last night that no one can leave. We're staying an extra night."

"So that means you don't have to leave today?" he asked, suddenly no longer angry at the brightness outside. Not if it meant more time with her.

She shook her head, smile beaming. "Wanna hang out with me?"

"Hell yes." He threw off the sheets and enjoyed her reaction to his nakedness. Her eyes widened and her lip sucked between her teeth as she smiled.

She giggled and jumped back into bed with him.

Best snow day ever.

THEY BARELY MADE it down to breakfast before closing time. Nathan was tempted to never leave the bed at all, but his body needed a little bit of recovery time. He was good, but he wasn't a machine.

Holly stopped at her room on their way down to the restaurant. She looked just as amazing in her dress as she did the first time around, although he preferred her messy sex-hair to the fancy up-do of the night before. The soft look fit her better.

"I'll be fast," she told him, unlocking the door. "I'll be right out. I'd let you in, but my roommate isn't feeling well. And I'm not sure she's dressed."

He leaned against the hallway door as she hurried inside. Gregory emerged from a shadow to check in with him.

"Hey," Nathan greeted him.

Gregory grunted.

"Yes, I had a fabulous night. And yes, she's amazing. No, she's not leaving today, and yes we will be going to the hot-spring later."

Gregory nodded, pleased that Nathan had gotten all the nuance out of his message.

"She's something else," Nathan said.

"I like her. She's good for you."

Nathan looked over at him surprised. "What do you mean?"

"You're smiling. I haven't seen you this happy in ages."

Nathan thought about it for a moment. "Maybe it's just because I got some."

Gregory shook his head. "This is different."

Nathan looked at him and Gregory grunted.

"What's that supposed to mean?" Nathan asked him. He couldn't always speak Gregory.

"There's 'I just got laid' happy, which granted, you have going on right now, and there's 'I'm actually legit happy,'" Gregory explained. "You have the legit happy look. It's different."

"And you can tell?" Nathan crossed his arms.

"I'm paid to watch you. It's my job to read your body language to better keep you safe." Gregory shrugged. "You're legit happy."

"Huh." Nathan leaned back against the wall, letting the back of his head rest on the wood.

He was happy. He hadn't thought about work for hours. The dread wasn't there. The worry, the anxiety, the ache for something more – none of it was there when he was around her.

Nathan chuckled. This is what he had wanted when he came here this weekend: peace. He hadn't expected to find it in the arms of the sexiest schoolteacher he'd ever met.

"You really like her?" Nathan asked Gregory.

Gregory grunted.

Nathan knew that one. It meant yes, in a completely non-sexual way.

"I like her, too. It feels like I've known her my whole life. I don't know how that is."

"Soul mates," Gregory supplied. "I'm not saying that's what it is, especially since you've known her for about twenty-four hours now."

"Soul mates?" Nathan grinned at his friend. "I didn't know you were a romantic, Gregory."

Gregory just grunted.

A few moments later the hotel room door opened. Gregory melted back into the shadows as Holly emerged. She'd brushed her hair, pulling it back into a ponytail with loose strands that framed her lovely face. She wore leggings and a soft looking sweater.

"I've got my swimsuit on and brought a change of clothes." She held up a small tote bag. "The lifts are closed for the day since there's so much snow, so we can't go skiing anyway. I'm looking forward to your idea of swimming after breakfast."

The idea of Holly in a swimsuit, the two of them alone in one of the pools, instantly cured him of any tiredness. He was ready to go again in an instant. He told himself to cool down. Breakfast first. Then more sex. And more sex. And more sex.

It seemed that the more he got of her, the more he wanted.

"I love that idea," Nathan replied, managing to keep his voice from betraying his lusty thoughts. "How is your roommate?"

"Better." Holly smiled at him. "Thanks for asking. I think she's finally got it out of her system. Now she's just glad we have an extra day so she can make it through a few more episodes of her show."

Nathan chuckled and together they walked down to breakfast.

The breakfast area was comfortably busy. Usually by this time of day the place was deserted as everyone had already hit the slopes, but with the lifts closed, that meant that everyone could linger over their breakfast and coffee.

Holly found a small table off to the side next to the fireplace and they both sat down.

"What can I get you?" a familiar voice asked.

Merryweather, with her strange knowing eyes and soft smile stood before them.

"You work here too?" Holly asked.

"We're short-staffed with the snow," Merryweather replied. "Can you believe how much we got? The weatherman says it's the snow of the century. Maybe even a couple of centuries. I think I believe him."

"It came down so fast," Holly said, looking out the window. "It almost feels like magic."

"Maybe it was." Merryweather's eyes twinkled. "Anyway, what can I get you? We have a full breakfast today."

"Waffles and coffee for me," Holly answered. She grinned at Nathan. "You were right about the waffles."

He chuckled. "Waffles and coffee for me as well. And orange juice."

"Coming right up," Merryweather said with a smile. She bustled off to the kitchen, weaving her way between tables and smiling at guests.

"So, can you believe there is so much snow the lifts are closed?" Holly shook her head. "It seems funny to me to be snowed in at a ski ranch and unable to ski."

Nathan chuckled. "Maybe we'll be stuck here for longer than just a day."

"I don't know." Holly scrunched up her nose, shaking her head. "It's almost Christmas. I would miss all the holiday fun."

Nathan had almost forgotten that it was Christmas. He now noticed the Christmas tree off to the side. There was a menorah in the window. An instrumental version of *Silver Bells* played overhead.

"Right. I forgot, you don't really do the holidays," Holly said.

"What if you came with me to San Francisco for the holiday?" Nathan wasn't sure where the request came from. It wasn't something he'd been thinking of, but the words just came right out. "I know it's not a traditional Christmas location, but I think you'd like it."

A soft smile crossed Holly's face, telling her she was considering it. Then she shook her head. "I can't. I promised to help with the school, the parade, and the store's party." Her smile faltered. "It's probably the last one, so I can't miss it."

"The last one?" Nathan asked, wondering what she meant. But, right then, Merryweather arrived with their food and drinks.

"Here you two go," she said, setting the food down in

front of them. Nathan's mouth began to water. He was hungry from their exertions.

They both dug into their breakfasts.

"These are so good," Holly moaned, pouring syrup onto her plate. She smiled. "Waffles always make me think of my mom and Christmas." She shook her head.

"Why's that?"

"When I was five or six, my mom decided that we needed to have waffles on Christmas morning, just like they do on TV. 'Santa' brought her a waffle iron and while we played with our new presents, she attempted waffles."

Her smile went distant.

"Were they good?"

"Oh god, no. They were a disaster." She chuckled. "The waffle iron melted. All we had were these melted black plastic hockey pucks. The smoke detectors were going off, the dog was barking, and my mom just stood there with a spatula laughing. We had Eggo waffles the next year. Now they're tradition."

"She sounds wonderful," Nathan said. He wouldn't mind meeting this woman. The thought made him pause. He'd known Holly for twenty-four hours and was already considering meeting her parents. In fact, he was *excited* about meeting her parents.

What was in these waffles?

"She was," Holly replied. Her smile remained, but her eyes saddened. She saw him looking at her and explained. "She died three years ago. Cancer."

Nathan suddenly felt horrible. "I'm so sorry."

"Thanks." She shrugged and put a smile back on. "This time of year it's hard not to think of her. All the books say to focus on happy memories. And there's just so many happy memories of her around Christmas."

"Like the waffles?"

"Yeah." She chuckled. "One year, she decided that our house wasn't festive enough. She wanted it covered in lights like one of those holiday Christmas cards. So, she spent hours outside hanging lights and nearly broke her neck on the ladder. She was so excited to turn them on, and when she did, only half of them worked."

"Oh no."

"She called it art," Holly laughed. "The next year, she took the same lights and spelled out 'Merry Christmas' on the lawn with them. It was great until the local teenagers came by and changed it into the shape of a giant penis."

Nathan couldn't help the immature chuckle that escaped him.

"She kept the penis. She added those decorative tree balls to the testicles. She didn't change it until the neighbors complained."

Nathan was starting to see where Holly's love of Christmas came from. It would be easy to love the holiday if he had memories like these.

"She would always just laugh about stuff. She loved anything to do with Christmas. It's how I got my name, even though I was born in July. She was the one who came up with the Christmas gifts at their bookstore. She felt it was really important to share the season of giving with the community. So she did."

"The gifts at the bookstore?" Nathan remembered she had mentioned something about a bookstore before. Her father owned one.

"My parents own a bookstore. Or my dad does now. Every year on Christmas day we hand out presents to all the kids that come in. It's become a town tradition. My dad dresses up like Santa and all the kids come and the parents hang out."

"That sounds amazing," Nathan said, feeling a twinge of

jealousy at something he'd never had. Something that he'd never thought he even wanted.

"Yeah." Her smile fell a little, but she shook her head. "Anyway, enough about me. What are your Christmas traditions? Do you make giant glowing dicks in your front yard too?"

Nathan laughed at the idea. "No. Christmas was never big in my house. I remember a couple of good Christmases with my mom, but then she died when I was little. My dad was never in the holiday spirit after that."

"Oh, I'm sorry." Holly looked down at her empty plate. "I wouldn't have asked if I had known."

"Then how would you have found out? Anyway, my dad kicked me out when I was sixteen. I discovered that I could make a lot of money working on Christmas because no one else wanted to. It just kind of stuck."

"So you don't really do anything for the holidays?" Holly asked, tipping her head and looking at him like he might be from a different planet.

"I do this." He motioned to the ski resort. "My company has a big party. Graham has an amazing party that I love going to every year."

She nodded thoughtfully, then smiled at him. "I'm glad I got to be a part of your Christmas traditions this year."

"Maybe I'll become a part of yours next year." He said it without thinking. The words just popped out.

Luckily, she just took it in stride. "That would wonderful. I promise not to make you waffles."

Nathan chuckled.

"You want to go to the hot-springs now? I mean, I know we're supposed to wait half-an-hour before swimming, but..." Holly shrugged and gave him a flirtatious grin.

"That sounds amazing."

Nathan stood and Merryweather was there to take their

plates. "You two have a marvelous day. Enjoy the magic of the snow."

Holly thanked her and Nathan made sure to leave a generous tip on the table. Then, he showed Holly to his private pool.

CHAPTER 17

*H*olly

WHEN NATHAN SAID that he had a private pool, Holly had assumed it would be something like a hot tub near the main pool, maybe slightly enclosed or with some potted plants making it more private.

She was wrong.

It was a private pool that was *very* private.

The resort's hot-spring river started at the base of the mountain and ended at the big swimming pool just outside the main building. A steaming creek meandered around the property with small ponds branching off at various locations as it snaked down toward the main pool. There were bigger public pools for up to ten people, and smaller quiet pools that fit three or four. Trees and bushes helped create the illusion that there was lots of space between the pools and gave some privacy. The best pools were gated off from the others, but the very best were hidden.

Nathan's was one of the hidden pools. If she hadn't seen him open the gate, she would have thought it was just another line of evergreen trees and not a separate area. Instead, she discovered they had their own private oasis.

The water pooled in a natural looking rock basin, but all the stones inside the pool were smooth and selected for comfort. She doubted nature made the pool quite this perfect, but who ever had designed it had kept to Mother Nature's aesthetics. Big flat stones surrounded the pool edge, making it easy to walk around. A large heated bench with an awning was the perfect place to hang a robe and towel and be sure it would be snow-free and dry. There was a small table with a button on it off to the far side of the enclosure.

Trees and shrubs hid the metal fencing, but they were done in such a way that it felt like she was out in the middle of the woods rather than just off the side of a hotel. Snow floated down, melting in the rising steam of the hot water.

"This is amazing," Holly whispered. She knew that Blue Aspen was fancy, but this took fancy to a whole new level. She pulled her hair up into a messy bun on the top of her head.

"Graham is mad that I rented it out before he did," Nathan told her with a chuckle. "It's an annual competition between us as to who can get to it first. He won last year, I got this year."

Nathan walked confidently across the stones to the bench and began stripping. The cold didn't seem to phase him as he pulled off his shirt, exposing bare skin to the snow.

Holly watched him for a second, enjoying the view. The man worked out. She remembered the way his broad shoulders felt on her hands when he was on top of her and a warm thrill went straight to the spot where her legs met.

Nathan looked good in his swim trunks. They were probably by some designer, but she liked the dark navy color on him and the way they hugged his hips. He sat on the edge of the pool, feet in the warm water, and looked over at her.

"You coming?"

She shook herself, making sure she wasn't drooling as she headed to the bench. Once there, she realized that there was an infrared heat lamp, so even the three steps from the bench to the pool would be in comfort. She wiggled out of her leggings and sweater, knowing that Nathan was watching her just as she had just watched him.

She rather liked the idea, so she made sure to give him a show.

He lounged on the far end of the pool, his eyes glued to her as she seductively walked across the stones and slid in. The warmth of the water enveloped her and she sighed and relaxed. She could feel her muscles loosen.

"I can see why this is your Christmas tradition," she said, staying low in the water so just her head peeked out. Snow flakes drifted down, catching in her hair and eyelashes before melting with the steam.

"Imagine skiing all day, and then coming to this," Nathan said, his voice inviting and low. "If I call or message the kitchen, they'll bring out food and drinks. They have these trays that hang over the water so you can eat without getting out."

The idea of eating in this warm, relaxing water sounded heavenly. "You better be careful," she teased him. "A girl could get used to this."

That's when she realized what she'd said. Again with wanting a future with him. She glanced over at him, but his eyes were closed and head back against a stone. He made a noncommittal noise and Holly hoped that it meant he hadn't really heard what she'd said.

She looked at him, putting him in her memory. The brown hair, spiky now with the falling snow and steam, the strong jaw, the confident nose, and the easy smile. He peeked open one chocolate brown eye at her and smiled, knowing she was looking at him.

"The view's better over here." He patted the stones next to him.

Heat that had nothing to do with the hot-spring flared again. A desire to strip from her swimsuit filled her. To feel him inside of her again. She knew that no matter how many times she had him, it would never grow old. It would be like cooking. There would always be something new and wonderful to try with him.

She grinned, catching her lower lip in a sultry smile as she made her way to him. Now that the dirty thoughts had entered her mind, she was going to use them. She only had a day left with him and she wasn't going to waste it.

Instead of sitting next to him, Holly moved to put her knees on either side of his hips. His eyes opened slowly as he found her straddling his waist. The reaction that she felt under the water said that he was as ready as she was.

"This is a private pool, right?" she asked him, the idea that someone might walk in on them making her slightly nervous. She didn't move though.

"Very private," he assured her, leaning forward and kissing the delicate spot where her jaw met her throat. She shivered with anticipation.

She reached behind her and unhooked her swim top. Slowly, she put it on the edge of the pool so it wouldn't float away with the current. Nathan's eyes dilated and his breath caught. He shifted his hips beneath her and she felt just how excited he was.

It was empowering to know that she had this kind of power over him. She inspired a physical reaction that he couldn't hide. That he didn't want to hide.

One that she would enjoy in just a few minutes.

CHAPTER 18

*N*athan

NATHAN HAD ALWAYS LOVED this pool. It wasn't just that he beat Graham to it, although that did make it sweeter. There was a peacefulness to this pool. A quiet. He felt serene and comfortable here. He'd spent many hours in this particular place, watching the sky and the water.

Today, it became cemented as his favorite place in the whole world.

And it was all because of Holly.

He'd loved watching her strip down to her cute little bikini. She seemed shy and slightly unsure of her body, but he found her absolutely stunning. She had curves. She was human and there wasn't a piece of plastic in her. It was a nice change from the Barbie-doll like women he'd found in California.

And then she took off her top and he forgot everything.

"Wow," he whispered, his eyes staring at the beauty in the water.

Holly grinned, looking sexy as hell.

"Do you have any idea what you do to me?" he asked her, moving his hands through the water to cup her breasts. She was so soft under his fingers that he nearly groaned.

She rocked her hips against him, her legs straddling his waist and this time he really did groan.

"Tell me," she said, lifting her arms up and putting them on his shoulders. "Tell me what I do to you."

"You turn me on." His fingers played with the swell of her breast before palming her completely. "You excite me. You drive me crazy."

He thrust his hips upward, wanting to be a part of her. If not for his swim trunks and her swim bottoms, he would have buried himself inside of her by now.

She grinned, pulling her lower lip between her teeth. "Then sit on the edge of the pool," she told him. She slid off of him, floating just out of his reach.

He did as she asked, hopping out and sitting on the flat edge of the pool. He chose to sit on the side with the heat lamp, so even though it was snowing, he didn't feel the cold. If anything, his back felt almost too warm.

Holly hummed softly, her head floating over the water as she came to his knees. She tugged on the hem of his swim trunks and waggled her eyebrows. He got the hint and lifted his hips so she could tug them free. She set them to the side.

He loved the little gasp she made when she saw him ready to go. He loved that she licked her lips and her pupils dilated. She smiled up at him, all bold and sure of herself.

And then she rose out of the water and kissed the tip of his erection. All ability for rational thought fled his brain as the rest of the blood in his body rushed south. She took him into her hands, kissing up and down his length.

He groaned, his head falling back and eyes rolling deep into his head. Every touch was better than the one before. She took him into her mouth, giving him warmth and sucking as she did so. He was sure he was going to explode into her mouth if she kept that up.

"Holly," he gasped, her tongue making him shiver and moan as she explored his length.

She looked up at him with big green eyes. To know that a woman as amazing as Holly would be willing to go down on him like this made him feel like a god. That a goddess like Holly would debase herself willingly for him was the biggest turn on he could imagine.

It took all his willpower to pull away. It felt so damn good, but he knew that if he let her continue, he would lose himself. He didn't want to do that yet. He wanted to enjoy this experience.

"Your turn," he told her. Her eyes widened in surprise. "Hop on out."

She pulled herself out of the water and onto the flat rock under the heat lamp. With a wiggle of her hips, she tugged at her wet swim bottoms until she stood gloriously naked before him.

Again, he was glad he had some self control, because he nearly blew at the sight of her. Somehow, she made him feel like a teenage boy. It was a testament to her sexiness.

"Where do you want me?" she asked, settling on the edge of the pool with her feet in the water.

"Right there," he told her, coming between her knees.

She swallowed hard as he shouldered her knees apart and licked his lips. Before him was a gourmet meal. He wanted to bring her to the cusp of madness before bringing her over the edge.

Slowly, teasing her with his fingers and kisses, he worked his way from her hip bone to her center. She whimpered as he touched her and she leaned back on her elbows, giving him better access.

He brought his mouth to the center of her arousal and began to explore with his tongue. He watched her stomach muscles contract as she arched into him, her moans filling the small space. He used every trick he knew with his teeth and tongue.

He brought her nearly to climax and pulled back, making her whimper and cry for more. He knew that when he did let her come, it would be powerful and intense. He brought her to the cusp of climax not once, but three times before finally flicking his tongue against her instead of pulling away when she began to pant.

Her spine arched and she came hard. It took the last remaining bits of his self control not to explode at the sight of her losing herself to him. It was erotic and sexy as hell. Her toes curled and her breath came in needy gasps as she shuddered and shivered beneath him.

Her body went limp as he pulled back, surveying the results of his work. Her cheeks were flushed and her eyes still rolled back in her head as she lay collapsed upon the stones. If not for her panting breath, he would have been afraid he killed her with pleasure.

Slowly, she leaned up on one elbow and looked at him. "I think it's your turn," she whispered.

He pulled himself out of the water and hurried to his pants. He pulled out the condom and slipped it on, turning to see she was still laying on the ground and smiling at him. She spread her legs, inviting him in.

She was warmer than the hot-spring and felt better than water ever could. Her legs wrapped around him and she moaned, arching her back to take him further into her. Every thrust was better than the last.

She became animated beneath him, rocking her hips and

writing to meet him. The animal in him took over, his brain fading into primal need. He wanted to fill her. To claim her.

Their mouths crashed together and the sticky wet of their warm skin and the water only added to the sensations beginning to overpower him. He was aware of only his body and how well she fit to him. It was as if she were made for him and him alone.

"Nathan," she gasped, her voice low and full of longing. Her eyes were bright and her cheeks flushed.

He lost it when she said his name. The last of his self control was gone. She undid him and he shattered into her, losing himself to her completely. His body dove deep, searching to complete himself and finding that he could. She in turn rose to meet him, her body responding to his in kind.

They lay breathless and panting, warmed by the heat lamp. He could feel wet raindrops from the melted snowflakes land on his back, but her heat beneath him kept him warm. Slowly, he rose, looking down at the most beautiful woman he'd ever met.

She smiled up at him and he kissed her. It was sweet compared to the frantic urgency of just a few moments prior. They didn't have to say a word. He pulled her to sitting, wrapping her up in his arms for a moment before they slid back into the water.

Snow fell all around him as he became fairly sure he had died and gone to heaven.

CHAPTER 19

$\mathcal{H}$olly

SHE FLOATED in the warm water, turning slightly as the current moved through the pool. Hot water flowed from the base of the mountain into the various pools. It then collected and made its way to the main pool before disappearing into a mountain stream. The effect was that there was always a slight current through the pools, keeping the clean water flowing.

She felt ridiculously light and happy. Beside her, Nathan floated as well, their bodies touching, then floating apart, then touching again. They floated in comfortable silence. Holly remembered her parents having the same kind of easy silence as they read together.

Just being in the same space made them happy. They didn't have to talk or be funny. They didn't have to perform. Just the act of existing was enough to make the other content. She'd never understood just how wonderfully peaceful it could be until now.

A large snowflake melted directly on her forehead and the water ran into her eyes. That was the only thing that affected her comfort. She sighed, setting her feet on the pebbly bottom of the pond and maneuvered into an upright position. Her wet hair stuck to her head until her shoulders where it began floating on the top of the water.

She looked up. The snow was slowing down. Bits of blue sky were visible. The flakes didn't fall as quickly now, and she was sure she could hear the hum of snowplows, even if they were only in her mind. Her time here was almost up.

She couldn't stay here in this little piece of heaven, no matter how much she wanted to. Eventually she had to go back home to her life. There were things that she couldn't abandon. Her father, her students, the bookstore, the town. Tomorrow, they would all have to come back.

She wondered what Nathan's life would go back to. Probably lots of meetings. Limousines. Expensive meals, but no time to eat them. To be a CEO was to be constantly working.

She knew the former owner of ECT, and George Element was constantly busy. It was a big reason why he sold the company to Paradigm. He was tired of the work and the energy required to keep everything running. She could only imagine what Nathan's job must be like if a smaller company was as difficult as George described.

She frowned. She wanted to spend more time with Nathan, how could she not, but how would she manage to fit into his life? George had been married and divorced twice in the past five years due to his job. He was never home, and the few times that he was, he was usually on his phone.

Nathan lived in San Francisco. She lived in Devonsville, CO. While Nathan probably had a private jet, she didn't. She barely had a savings account where he had to have multiple banks store his money. He was purchasing the company that would forever change her town, and not necessarily for the better.

The more she thought about it, the more it felt like this was a magical weekend in time where they could be together. After this, it probably wouldn't work. They were just too different.

"You look like you're thinking deep thoughts," Nathan said. She turned to see that he too had sat up. His dark hair steamed with heat from the water as he settled himself against a rock. She felt like she could look at him all day.

"Just thinking."

"A dangerous pastime," he replied.

"I know." She giggled. "You look like you've been thinking, too."

"Well, it did take some time for the blood to come back up to my brain, but yes," he smiled. She liked the way his eyes softened when he looked at her. His face had a hardness, but it disappeared whenever he focused on her. She liked that.

"Penny for your thoughts," she offered. "I know you don't need it, but it's all I can afford right now."

He chuckled. "I was thinking about Christmas traditions," he said after a moment. His dark eyes found hers. "And possibly trying out a new one."

Her eyebrows raised. "And?"

"Come with me to San Francisco." He leaned forward and took her hands in his. "We don't have to stop here. Come back with me."

It was a tempting offer. Too tempting, really. If it were any other time but Christmas, she would have said yes in a heartbeat. Despite how different their worlds were, she still wanted to be with him.

"I can't." She hated the words coming out of her mouth. "I want to, but I can't. What about after Christmas?"

Hurt filled Nathan's eyes but he quickly blinked it away. "I can't do after Christmas," he told her. "Business picks up then. I won't have any spare time. I don't want to do that to you."

She hated the bitterness that filled his voice. He sighed leaning back against the pond walls, but still holding onto her hands under the water.

"What if you come home with me?" she asked him. "I'll make you Eggo waffles. You can see the bookstore. I think you'd love it."

He dropped her hands. "I can't. There's too much work to be done. In California, I can bring you to work. I can multi-task. I can't do that if I go with you."

"You're going to work over Christmas?" she asked him.

"I always do. It's what I've always done. It's why I'm successful," he said, a touch of anger creeping into his voice. "And I've delegated too much as it is. My business runs my life. You need to know that."

She did. She could already see how this relationship would go. They were on vacation now. It wouldn't work in the real world. They both had too much work and were each too devoted to it. It was something they shared.

Holly's chest felt heavy and full of dark clouds. This wasn't how she wanted to spend her last day with him. She wanted to float and laugh again. She wanted to see him smile. She didn't want to bring up his past or hers and make things ache. They didn't have enough time together to fix these things.

They just had today.

"Let's talk about this later," she said, knowing that wasn't going to happen. "I don't want to bring us down. Not when I'm having the best day ever."

A half smile attempted to form on his face. "Best day ever?"

She grinned at him. "Definitely top ten. You get me lobster for dinner and maybe another round in your bed, you'll make top five for sure."

He gave her a cocky grin. "I can do better than lobster," he told her.

"And the bed part?"

"Why don't we go upstairs and see?"

CHAPTER 20

*M*erryweather

"SHE'S GOING TO LEAVE," Flora said, frowning at the sky. "Maybe we should make more snow."

Merryweather sighed. "We can't make more snow," she told her sister. "And it's okay that she leaves. We just need to make sure that he chases her."

Flora's frown slowly faded. "And you have a plan?"

"Do I have a plan?" Merryweather scoffed. "Dear sister, I always have a plan."

Flora snorted.

"Fine. *This* time I have a plan," Merryweather replied, ignoring her sister's eye roll. "I have a wonderful Christmas-inspired plan."

CHAPTER 21

*N*athan

NATHAN WISHED the night would go on forever. He wished that the dawn would never come. If he had the power, he would have frozen time so that he and Holly could stay in this moment forever.

But he had money, not power over time, and dawn came as expected.

He lay in bed, his eyes closed against the sunlight, his arms wrapped tightly around the woman of his dreams. He didn't know how she did it, but she just got better and better.

They'd talked all night when they weren't busy exploring and enjoying one another's bodies. She made him laugh. She'd listened when he spoke. She told him of her favorite books and why she loved to teach. When he told her things, she nodded and understood. Never once throughout the night did he feel judged or inadequate. Now that it was morning, he found himself wishing they had another day.

Usually, he was already out the door and forgetting their names by now.

But not Holly. Holly was different. The way she smiled at him was real. The way she laughed at his jokes was sincere, especially because she didn't laugh at all of them. He loved the way she looked at him when she thought he couldn't see.

Was it possible to fall in love with someone in just hours?

He sighed. She wouldn't come to San Francisco before Christmas. He'd tried a couple more times, but she was firm. She had a community that depended on her. Responsibilities at home. There was apparently a parade and of course her father's Christmas party.

He was sincerely considering having her come out after the holidays. He could probably get away between meetings. He could pass more tasks on to Lucy. That thought made him grimace. He gave her too much of his responsibility as it was. She had done so much of the work around combining these tech companies. He didn't doubt her abilities, but it did make him nervous how much power he was giving her.

That made him think of Holly's request to look into ECT. He'd given that company to Lucy. It was supposed to be his responsibility, but he had so many things on his plate with RentTech. A move was a big decision. He didn't remember approving the company to move, but given how stressed he'd been this past month, it was a possibility.

Either way, it was concerning. He was going to have to look into things as soon as he got home. Lucy did a good job, but she wasn't hired for this kind of thing. He needed to make sure she wasn't overstepping her boundaries.

The thought made him tired. He'd needed this weekend getaway more than he realized. He was tired. The job exhausted him. He didn't really want to go back, to be honest, but he didn't know what else to do.

Money was everything. This was his job. This was where his money came from.

Before he could give it more thought, the beautiful woman sleeping beside him stirred. She sighed with contentment, nuzzling her head onto his shoulder. She fit like a long lost puzzle piece.

"Good morning," she whispered, her voice husky with sleep.

"Good morning," he agreed. He stroked her soft hair with his fingers, memorizing the way she looked. If nothing else, this weekend had been good for his soul.

"What time is it?" Holly asked, purposefully not opening her eyes. "Tell me it's midnight and not morning."

"It's midnight and not morning," he repeated dutifully.

She chuckled and opened one beautiful green eye to look at him.

"It's a little past nine. We still have time."

Checkout was soon. She was leaving then to avoid the traffic and get home before dark. He had things he needed to do today as well.

She sighed, this time with disappointment. "Did it snow more?"

He shook his head. He'd already checked. The roads were clear. It was a beautiful Monday morning and the sun was shining. It was supposed to be a beautiful day.

"Maybe you could call in sick?" he offered.

"Tempting," she told him, nestling back into his shoulder. "But I'm out of sick days. Plus, it's the last week of school before break. The kids are expecting me. I can't."

He admired her dedication, even if it meant less time. It didn't matter anyway. They were just pretending at this relationship thing anyway.

He wasn't meant for happiness like that.

He sighed. The magic of the weekend was wearing away.

Soon, he too would have to return to work. It was a beautiful escape to a dream, but they both knew it was time to wake up.

She kissed the curve of his shoulder. He turned to see her green eyes smoldering and a hopeful grin filling her face.

"You said we still have time," she said, moving to kiss him. "Lets make the most of it."

And so they did.

HOLLY STOOD by the door of the lobby, feet frozen in place. Her bag lay at her feet.

"I don't want to go," she whispered, looking back at him. "It was such a good weekend."

Nathan kissed her forehead. "I'll call you."

She smiled, but her eyes said she didn't believe him. Why should she? This was a vacation fling. This wasn't supposed to be serious.

She picked up her bag. "You'll look into why Paradigm is moving ECT to San Francisco, right?"

He nodded. "Yes. I will."

She paused, seemingly looking for any way to prolong leaving. An old beat-up four-door sedan pulled up to the front door. It looked out of place among the expensive cars waiting for the valet. The car didn't belong here. Just like Holly.

"Thank you for the most amazing weekend," Holly said. She set her bag down and stood in front of him. "It was like a dream."

She went to her tip-toes and kissed him softly on the mouth. She still tasted sweet and made his heart race. He closed his eyes, focusing on her taste and the soft scent of her.

When he opened them she was gone. The old car pulled away, rumbling and sputtering into the snow.

"You okay, Boss?" Gregory asked, appearing out of the ether.

Nathan grunted. Gregory understood. That was his natural language after all.

"You just seem..." Gregory searched for the right word. "Unhappy again."

"Again?" Nathan asked, his eyes going to his bodyguard.

"You were whistling yesterday. You only do that when you're actually happy."

"Tell Hal I apologize." His eyes searched the road for Holly's car. "It was her."

Gregory's eyes followed Nathan's gaze. "So find a way to get her. You're rich. You can do it. You should be happy."

"It's not that simple." Nathan rolled his eyes, but Gregory was gone. Back into the shadows. Protecting him from everything but himself.

Nathan sighed. He went back to his room. He could go skiing. He could go swimming. There was an amazing gym on site, but that didn't appeal to him either. He wasn't hungry, but he did consider getting drunk. But even that didn't sound like something he wanted to do.

He shook his head. He shouldn't feel like this. He knew her for two days. Two days. It was ridiculous to feel like he'd just lost half his body when she walked away. It was crazy to have this ache in his chest.

Yet, there it was.

He stood at the window, staring out at the clear skies and crisp snow on the mountain. The lifts were up and running again, and skiers and snowboarders raced down the mountain. He watched them for a few minutes, his mood continuing to sour.

He needed to change his thoughts. He needed to make

himself feel better. So, he did the one thing that had made him feel good since he was sixteen.

He checked his bank account.

When Nathan opened his first bank account, he had a grand total of one hundred three dollars and twenty-seven cents. He'd saved for weeks to buy a decent computer, and from there started building his computer programs. He made money.

Everything snowballed from that first computer program sale. Paradigm had scooped him up. Now there were board members, stock holders, and thousands of employees. With success came more work. But, he'd learned long ago that work meant money. And money was what he craved.

He'd loved starting his company, but somewhere along the line, the money made became more important than creating. Money became the guidepost. Money was the reward, and money was the goal. Money never made him feel worthless or small.

There were days where it felt like he would never succeed, yet when he looked at the money he'd made, he felt better. After a few years, the hundreds turned to thousands and he was happy. The thousands turned into hundreds of thousands. He had to start adding up his bank accounts, and he was happy. Then millions. And he was happy.

The day his accounts said one billion dollars was one of the best days of his life.

Nathan opened his phone and pulled up his accounts. He was lower today due to some market fluctuations but he sat at just over the billion mark. He waited for the feeling of accomplishment and peace to flow through him like it always did.

But nothing happened.

He clicked through some of the accounts, making sure to pick ones that would show him his wealth.

And no rush of joy followed. No pride. No joy.

Today, it was just numbers.

This had never happened before. The money was why he worked so hard. It was why he barely slept. It was the reason he tolerated the office and the meetings. It was the money, not the work that drove him.

And today the money didn't matter.

"Screw it," he said, tossing the phone to the side. He slouched into a chair, more grumpy now than before.

With angry jerky motions, he went to his laptop and pulled it open. He needed something to distract him. He pulled up the reports and files on Elements Computer Technologies.

The company was a good purchase. The owner and CEO wanted out. He was selling for a good price. He dug a little deeper. ECT was based out of a town in Northern Colorado called Devonsville. A college nearby fed into the company, providing new local talent.

The company and the college were the two biggest employers in the county. The town prospered and fed into the success of ECT. Yet, it was still considered a medium sized company and a tiny player in the world of computer technology.

Nathan leaned back in his chair, putting his hands behind his head. Why were they moving this company to San Francisco? He'd let Lucy handle the majority of this as he'd been busy handling the fiasco with RentTech. He'd barely looked at this since it wasn't going up in flames.

But now that RentTech was no longer on the evening news, it was time to look into this. He picked up his phone again and dialed Lucy.

"What's up, boss-man?" she asked on the second ring. "How's the vacation going?"

"Why are we moving Element Computer Technologies to California?" He didn't bother explaining more.

"ECT? Why do you want to know about them?" Lucy asked. He could hear her typing in the background.

"It's my job," Nathan replied. "Now that I've survived RentTech, I need to keep my momentum. The board isn't happy. I need to provide a win."

"ECT is moving to California for better talent. Paradigm attracts the best, but as ECT is remaining a subsidiary, it still needs more mojo," Lucy answered. "Plus, there's a tax break incentive."

"How is a tech company the size of Paradigm getting a tax break incentive?" Nathan asked. That didn't make much sense.

"It's a small business tax incentive," Lucy said, sounding proud of herself. "ECT is small enough to qualify, even as a subsidiary. We'll save millions by moving the company here."

Nathan tried to ignore the twitch in his chest. He'd done worse things for money.

"And it's legal?" Nathan asked her.

"I wouldn't have done it if it wasn't," Lucy assured him. "Millions, Nathan. You said money comes first."

He nodded. That was his motto: money comes first. Money was everything.

"You okay, boss?" Lucy asked. "You don't sound like you. Normally, the talk of millions has you all smiles."

Nathan didn't know how to answer her. He pulled up the upcoming plans for ECT. The former CEO and some of his executives were supposed to be flying in to meet with him on Wednesday.

An idea started to form, along with a smile.

"Lucy, I want you to cancel George Element's flight tomorrow," he told his secretary.

"Um, sure. What do you want me to tell them is the reason why? And I'll make sure to cancel the meeting."

"No, the meeting is still on. It's just that I'm coming to them," Nathan explained. "I'm only a couple of hours away right now. No need for a flight."

"Okay." Lucy drew out the syllables, obviously unsure what her boss was doing. "That's not usually your move, but sure. I can move the meeting to... Devonsville. Wow. Middle of nowhere."

Nathan barely heard the disdain in Lucy's voice. He was already planning. Not only would he get to inspect the company first hand, he'd get to see Holly.

It wasn't sound business to mix business and pleasure, but for the first time in his life, Nathan didn't care if it cost him a little bit of money.

That, if nothing else, surprised him. Money was everything.

"Are you sure about this, Nathan?" Lucy asked. "Are you really sure you're feeling okay?"

"I'm feeling better than I have in weeks," Nathan assured her. "Just make the changes."

"Okay. You're the boss." Lucy's shrug was practically audible. "I'm just telling you it's not a good idea."

"Thank you, Lucy. Just do it."

The line was quiet for a moment. Then the keys clacked. "It's done." Lucy's voice was sullen and low.

But Nathan didn't care.

He hung up on Lucy and went back to evaluating ECT. It was like stepping back in time to when he first started his own business. The little things about the company fascinated him. He had so many plans just by looking. He hadn't been this excited in years.

And his excitement wasn't even including the prospect of seeing Holly again.

CHAPTER 22

*H*olly

"YOU SEEM... SAD." Aliyah glanced over from the passenger seat, her dark eyes looking Holly over like she was worried her friend might be sick.

Holly kept her eyes on the road. Aliyah had gotten the car from the lot, but Holly was driving home.

"Was it that guy?" Aliyah pressed. "You were pretty happy yesterday."

"Yeah." Holly sighed. "Have you ever connected with someone immediately? Like, you don't even need to know them for more than an hour to like them?"

"Sure." Aliyah leaned back in her seat. "I liked you the moment I met you."

Holly smiled at the memory. On her very first day as a teacher at Devonsville Elementary, Holly had been over-whelmed and nervous. She was worried that everyone would think she'd gotten the job because of her father rather than her education and experience.

Aliyah had plopped down next to her in the lunch room. "We're now room buddies," Aliyah informed her. "And I have a feeling we're going to be friends, too."

Aliyah had always been a good friend.

"Did you feel that with this guy? I need a name for him, by the way. And some details." Aliyah crossed her arms and glared at her friend.

"His name is Nathan. And yes. I did."

"Then why are we driving away? If you feel something, you should go with it."

"This isn't a romance novel," Holly chided. "He's not going to sweep me away to his castle and everything will be sunshine and roses. He has a job. One that keeps him stupid busy. I have a job."

"One that keeps you stupid busy?"

Holly narrowed her eyes at her.

"Yes. My job at the school and at the bookstore are important. We're just too different. We talked about it. It wasn't going to work. Our lives were just too busy."

"So, it was just really amazing vacation sex?"

"I guess it was." Holly felt empty at the words. "It was just vacation sex. Besides, he hates Christmas."

"Well, then I know he's not the one for you," Aliyah said. "You made the right choice then. It wouldn't work out between you. You love Christmas."

Holly nodded, but she found herself missing Nathan already. How was it possible to miss someone she'd only known for two days? Somehow, it felt like she'd known him her whole life.

She sighed. She needed to stop thinking about Nathan. He was gone. The weekend was just a wonderful weekend. Nothing more.

"So, you hungry?' Holly asked, pulling onto the highway and away from the resort.

"Actually, I am," Aliyah replied with a smile.

"I'll stop at the next gas station for sandwiches." Holly grinned at her, wide and as annoying as possible.

"It will be a shame when I murder you," Aliyah said, shaking her head.

DEVONSVILLE SAT JUST off the main interstate about an hour from the Wyoming border and two hours from Denver. The state college was only a few miles away, and as a result the town had a fun college age appeal. Many of the houses were rented out to college students as they were cheaper here than closer to campus, but the students kept them in good repair.

There were lots of small restaurants and a lively down-town with bars and shops. Students liked to bring their parents to Devonsville when they came to visit for the fancier meals and the parents stayed in Devonsville for the cheaper hotels.

Lights adorned the trees, though there seemed to be less of them this year. The news that ECT was leaving was hurting the town. Houses were going up for sale. Several businesses were closing as spouses prepared to move.

Holly's apartment was cold and empty when she arrived home. She'd dropped Aliyah off at her house and now was on her own. Her small building was a modified motel with outside entrances. Holly kept a small potted plant on the porch, but it was long dead with the winter. The sun had already set and the sky was cold and gray. Holly wondered if it was going to snow again.

She hoped so. White Christmases were always nice.

Holly walked up the steps to her apartment, kicking the

dirty parking lot snow from her shoes as she unlocked the front door.

"Oh good, you're home." Mrs. Krasinski popped her head out of the apartment next door. Mrs. Krasinski was a retired housewife with too much time on her hands some days. "These arrived for you. I didn't want them to get too cold, so I brought them in."

Holly frowned. She hadn't ordered anything recently, though a relative could have sent something.

Mrs. Krasinksi's door opened and she stepped out carrying a beautiful vase full of roses and lilies. Holly's eyes opened wide in surprise.

"I didn't order this," Holly stammered. "Are you sure it's for me?"

"It's got your name on it," Mrs. Krasinski replied. She handed the vase off to Holly. "I think you might have a secret admirer."

Holly set the vase down on her welcome mat and reached for the card nestled in the flowers. She wondered if Mrs. Krasinski had already read it, and figured she had.

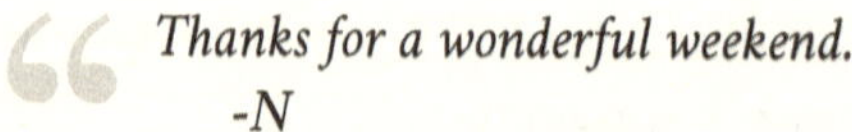

Thanks for a wonderful weekend.
-N

A SMILE FILLED Holly's face as her heart warmed. She picked up the vase and took a deep breath in of the flowers. They smelled sweet and fresh and as far from winter as she could imagine.

"So, who are they from?" Mrs. Krasinski pressed.

Holly smiled at her, kicking her bag inside the door. "You were right. A secret admirer."

She waved to her neighbor and shut the door, cradling the flowers to her chest. She set the vase on her small kitchen table, admiring how the flowers already made her apartment feel warmer.

She shook her head, smiling at the flowers. She wasn't sure what Nathan was doing by sending her these. It was probably just a nice gesture, and one she did appreciate.

Holly shrugged out of her jacket, hanging it on a chair, and then hit the thermostat up a couple of degrees. She couldn't afford to go too high, but it was too cold to be comfortable even with a sweater on.

Her phone rang, and for one hopeful moment, Holly thought it might be Nathan.

Instead it was her father.

"Holly! Are you back home? How was your trip?" Her father's voice crackled over the phone and she smiled.

"Hi, Dad. The trip was awesome," she told him. "I got to go skiing, and the hot-springs at Blue Aspen are just as amazing as everyone says they are."

"Oh honey, I'm so glad." She could hear him smiling. "And the award? How was that?"

Holly thought about the small statue tucked into her bag, but that wasn't really what she remembered about that night. She wasn't about to tell her father about Nathan, though.

"It was great. The food was amazing and there was an open bar," she said instead. "Oh, and remember that band, The Tones? They were the music for the night."

"I saw them in concert once. They were pretty good."

"How are you doing, Dad? You survive the weekend without me?" Holly put the phone on speaker mode and picked up her bag to start putting things away. She carried everything into the bedroom and plopped it on her bed.

"It was quiet. I was hoping for better, but..." He sighed. "I'm sure I'll sell everything off after Christmas."

Holly hated the defeat in his voice. The bookstore was her father's dream. He and her mother had opened it before Holly was born. Holly had grown up walking among the shelves of stories. She'd spent more of her life in that store than she had at home.

And it was closing. Her father had thought that e-books would be a passing trend and that he shouldn't change because of it. That had been a rough time, too. He'd nearly closed then, but he opened up a coffee shop and reading area. He expanded into business books. When he did that, things started looking up again. But, then the news of ECT leaving Devonsville hit. The majority of his money came from supplying technical books for ECT offices.

The loss of ECT was the store's death knell. She'd spent the last three months desperately trying to change that, but nothing she did seemed to matter. Without ECT's purchases, and their large customer base, the store was no longer viable.

It was the end of an era.

Holly's father hadn't announced the closure yet. Holly secretly thought he was hoping for a Christmas miracle. The plan was to announce it at the end of the Christmas party. He would give out his last books and presents. Then everything would go on sale and the business would close at the end of the year.

"It'll work out," Holly told her dad.

"Yeah." He had enough money that losing the store wouldn't bankrupt him. "I was actually thinking I might travel."

The idea of her father traveling made Holly laugh. The man hated being in the car longer than ten minutes. He couldn't stand airplanes, boats, or trains. He traveled by reading books.

"That sounds like a great idea," Holly told him. They both

knew it wasn't true. But, it was better to sound optimistic about the future than worrying and being sad.

It's what Holly's mother would have done.

"Well, I'll let you go and unpack. I'm sure you're tired from skiing all weekend."

Holly was tired, but it wasn't from skiing.

"Thanks for the call, Dad," Holly said, pushing thoughts of Nathan from her mind.

"I love you, kiddo."

"I love you too," she replied, a smile on her face.

They both hung up and Holly stood in her room. It was still cold.

Holly grimaced and put on fluffy pajamas and curled up in bed. The blankets slowly warmed as she grabbed a book. She held the book in her hands, looking like she was reading, but the words just kept sliding past without absorbing. Her thoughts were on Nathan.

She missed him. She wasn't sure how it was possible to miss someone she barely knew, but she did. She ached to have him in bed with her, reading his own book.

She sighed and put the book down. She turned off the light.

She had a busy day tomorrow. She might as well be well-rested for it.

CHAPTER 23

*H*olly

HOLLY WOKE a full hour before her alarm went off. She lay in bed with the covers up to her chin. Her cheeks were cold, but she didn't want to turn the heat up. The old apartment building leaked warm air like a sieve and her heating costs were already too high this year. Better just to wear an extra sweater. Or stay in bed.

She heard her coffee-pot click on, the machine on automatic. Soon the scent of coffee filled the air and she found the siren's song of endless energy irresistible. She slid out from under the covers, wrapped a robe around her and shuffled into the kitchen.

The sun was still barely cresting the horizon, and the kitchen was full of shadows. Holly went on autopilot, reaching for a mug, the creamer, and finally the coffee. She sighed with contentment at the first sip.

And then she thought of Nathan.

He liked his coffee with sugar, no cream.

She shook her head. It didn't matter how he liked his coffee. He was probably back in San Francisco by now. She wondered if he would look into ECT for her like she asked. She didn't doubt that he would, just that anything would come of it.

She glanced at her phone to see if there were any new messages or updates, but the screen held nothing but a new like on a Facebook post. She sipped on her coffee and started the shower, telling herself to get on with day and stop thinking of a man she was never going to see again.

"It was a dream," she told herself. "A marvelous dream, but it wasn't real."

With a sigh that came straight from her soul, she put down her coffee and got ready.

She arrived at school the required thirty minutes before the first bell. She wore comfortable slacks and a fluffy white and red sweater. She was glad she didn't have to pay for the heat at school, because for the first time all morning she finally felt warm.

She went around the room, putting the graded writing assignments on each student's desk. Today they would be transferring the now fixed paragraphs to handmade snowflakes and hanging them around the classroom. In a few hours, her room would look like a frosted paper winter wonderland.

"Ms. Jones?"

Holly looked up to see the school secretary in her door. Ms. Chellie handled everything that came through the front door of the school from attendance to packages to the new swing set they'd ordered last year.

"Hi. Is someone going to be absent today?" Holly asked,

standing up from her desk. Ms. Chellie didn't usually come by in person to inform her of an absence, but it happened from time to time.

"Nope. These came for you." Ms. Chellie stepped to the side, letting in a delivery man. The man had a vase bursting with the most beautiful red and white roses Holly had ever seen. It was massive, with sprigs of holly poking out among greenery between the roses.

"Just put them on my desk," Holly told the man. "I'll get you a tip."

"No need, ma'am," the delivery man replied. "It was included in the purchase. Have a wonderful day."

He tipped his hat and hurried out of the classroom. Ms. Chellie glanced out the door to make sure he really was leaving before coming over to admire the flowers.

"Holy cow," Chellie whispered. "I didn't know they made vases this big. Or flowers like this."

Holly reached for the pretty red card sitting carefully on the top of the flowers.

HAPPY TUESDAY

-N

THE SMILE that filled Holly's face was slow, but permanent. She had a feeling that it wouldn't go away for the rest of the day. There was something wonderful about knowing that someone was thinking of her. It was a great way to start a day.

"Who's N?" Chellie asked, peeking over Holly's shoulder. "And does he have a brother? Cousin? Good friend?"

Holly laughed. "I met him up the award thing," she explained.

Chellie took a deep breath in of the flowers and shook her head. "I think you did more than just meet. You made some sort of impression. Especially since this isn't all he sent."

Holly frowned. "What do you mean?"

Chellie grinned. "The library just got a delivery notice. Apparently, they're getting two 3D printers and a bunch of state of the art virtual reality learning gear. The nurse had to come in because all the librarians were hyperventilating they were so excited."

Holly's mouth dropped open. "What?"

"It's a donation from Paradigm Technologies. But, given the size of those flowers, I'm guessing that's where 'N' works," Chellie said with a knowing smile.

Holly didn't know what to say to that.

"You must have made an impression. I hope you got his number. He sounds like a keeper."

Chellie gave Holly a friendly pat on the back before returning to the front office. Students would be arriving soon. Holly stood staring at the flowers, trying to figure out why Nathan would send such an amazing gift.

It was meant for her. She knew it. Even though it was addressed to the school, it was a gift to her. She was a teacher and he sent her something she could only dream of to help her teach. He'd picked the perfect gift. The flowers were nice, but her students and school were the way to her heart.

"What is he doing?" Holly said aloud to the empty classroom. Probably just being nice. It cost his company very little to send this kind of thing and they would get a great tax deduction for it.

She barely had enough time to send him a thank you text before her students came running in. Everyone was red nosed and had snow on their boots, but they were all happy to see her.

"Ms. Jones! Ms. Jones!" they all called. "We had a snow-day yesterday!"

Holly laughed, greeting them and getting everyone settled at their desks. The mornings were always high energy, and today was no different. With the snow-day on Monday, there was only three days of school this week. Friday was the town holiday parade and celebration, so the school year ended on Thursday.

The classroom buzzed with energy. The kids were still amped up from their day off and the rumors of cool things happening in the library. They kept wanting to smell Holly's flowers and asked her a million questions as to where she got them, who sent them, what she was going to do with them, and if there were bees inside of them.

Holly took it all in stride. She loved being a teacher and this was part of it. It took a while, but she managed to settle them at their desks and to look over their writing assignments. It was easy to get them to work on making paper snowflakes. She handed out paper and scissors and let the kids follow their imaginations.

The snowflakes were a cleverly disguised learning opportunity. They'd already talked about the science of freezing water, but cutting the flakes let Holly introduce some geometry and math concepts.

When everyone had a snowflake they were proud of, they quietly worked on transferring their corrected holiday wishes onto their snowflake.

When lunch came around, Holly hung the snowflakes on the walls. She walked around, reading each child's wish. Many asked that their parents didn't need to move. Others asked for toys, puppies, and various dreams. Holly wished she could grant every single one of these wishes.

For the millionth time that day, she thought of Nathan.

Was he looking into the business relocation? What was he doing now? Was he back in California thinking of her?

She checked her phone for a reply to her thank you, but there was none. She tried not to pout as she slid the phone back into her desk. He was a busy business owner. She sighed and went back to work.

THE CHILDREN RUSHED out the door as soon as the bell rang. Coats and scarves flew in the wind and several gloves scattered the hallways. A lone snow-boot waited by the door. Holly dutifully went around and picked up the various items, knowing that tomorrow children would look for them in the lost and found.

She cleaned up the classroom and finished grading the math worksheet. With the end of the year so close, the kids were having a hard time concentrating on anything that didn't mention Santa or was made of candy.

Holly left the school, giving a wave to Chellie in the office, and headed to her father's bookstore. She parked on a side street and walked down Main Street to the large, red brick building.

The bookstore was an old building on the corner of Main Street and Oak Lane in the heart of downtown Devonsville. A family-owned Italian restaurant sat to the right, and a ice cream shoppe to the left. Everything was decorated for the holidays. Christmas-tree lights sparkled in the windows over carefully arranged books and gift ideas.

The door chimed softly as she walked inside. The soft scent of paper and books mingled with fresh coffee and right out of the oven chocolate chip cookies. It was the smell of home. She took a deep breath in and smiled, feeling content.

"Anything interesting happen today?" her father asked from his perch at the checkout lane.

Mark Jones was a man in his early sixties. He wore dark rimmed glasses over green eyes that matched Holly's and the two also shared a nose. His hair was gray now but cut short to hide just how gray.

"Two dragons and a flock of flying bananas," she replied, coming over and kissing his cheek. Mark smiled and laughed. It was a game they'd played ever since she was a little girl. He would ask if anything happened at school, and she would make up fantastical stories. "How's business?"

"Fine," he replied. There were only a couple of customers browsing the books, but the coffee shop was comfortably busy. "Let me get someone over here and we can go to the back to work on things."

Mark motioned to a teen-aged girl to come take his place at the cash register. Holly smiled her. The job at the book-store was a coveted position around town. Mark always hired the local teens, but he made them submit real resumes and held interviews. Even if it was just for a entry-level, part-time position, he wanted them to be prepared for the real world.

Holly and her father went upstairs and to Mark's office. The leather love-seat was worn and thin, but still her favorite place to take a nap. Books filled the room and the window let in the late afternoon sun.

A large piece of paper with the parade route sat ready on the desk. Holly pulled out fresh paper and pens for them to continue their planning.

She tried not to think that this was the last time they'd do this. She loved this time spent with her father. They'd designed so many parade floats in this room. She'd wrapped so many presents for the Christmas party. This was a room of fond memories.

And it was going to end. She pushed the heartache away.

"Let's get to work," she said, opening up a pen. Her father smiled and together, they bent their heads over his desk and planned.

CHAPTER 24

*N*athan

LUCY HAD CHOSEN him a local hotel, one of the big-chains, and rented out several rooms on the top floor. Hal and Gregory weren't fans of the security situation, but as a middle-sized town, there weren't many other hotel options. He could stay in Denver, but that was over an hour's drive away.

Nathan stood in his hotel room and looked around. The room had a decent sized living area that connected to the bedroom and bath. There was a big-screen TV and a comfortable couch. The bed was a queen with fluffy pillows.

It felt tiny and cheap to Nathan after the luxury of Blue Aspen. He knew it was still a nice hotel room. He'd just grown used to his wealth.

His father's words echoed in his mind. He'd grown soft. He was now one of *them*. He spent too much money. He should stay someplace cheaper. He didn't deserve even this level of comfort.

Nathan shook his head, trying to clear his father's voice from his mind. His father loved money, but hated spending it. Nathan had the same love of money, it was just that he had so much of it, he could afford to spend some.

"Sir, your car is here," Hal announced. "Would you like me to tell the driver to go around again?"

Nathan shook his head. "No, I'm ready." He checked his watch. He was right on time for the meeting with the Element Computer Technologies group.

Gregory was waiting with the dark windowed car. Nathan had requested not to have a limo, opting for a more economical and less visible vehicle. Gregory took the passenger seat next to the driver. Hal flowed behind in a second car.

Nathan gazed out the window, taking in the view. The Rocky Mountains stood with white peaks and heads in the clouds to the west. The town itself was picturesque. A cute downtown area with shops and restaurants. Nathan thought he saw a sign for "The Book Bag" but the car turned down a different street.

ECT headquarters was located at the northern end of town. Several large buildings sat around a man-made lake that had frozen over. It looked like an average high-end business location.

Nostalgia hit Nathan hard in the chest. Paradigm Technologies had looked like this at one point. A nice building with room to grow, but comfortable. He found himself missing those early days. He'd made more than enough to be comfortable, but the challenge was still there. He knew his employees then.

These days, he was so busy with board meetings, investor meetings, and the unending slog of emails requiring his constant attention that he no longer created technologies anymore. It had been ages since he'd even built his own computer. He just didn't have time for it anymore.

The irony that the king of tech didn't know what kind of video card he used was not lost on him. His fingers itched to touch a motherboard again. Ideas swirled in his mind for ways to improve function and speed, but he knew he'd never get to play with them.

He had meetings to attend.

He thought of Holly and wondered what she was up to today. He had to do the meeting first. Then he could go and surprise her. Business before pleasure, no matter how much he wanted the pleasure. Yet, it was just another thing that he couldn't do. One more limitation.

He sighed and rested his head against the cold glass of the window. He pulled out his phone and checked his bank account. Up one million today. The thrill was small. He put his phone away still unhappy with the work before him.

What was he going to do if this kept happening? It was the money that drove him. It was the thrill of seeing his bank accounts go up. He did everything possible to keep that happening. The last month with the RentTech fiasco bringing his numbers down had nearly destroyed him.

"Sir?" Gregory turned around in his seat.

Nathan looked at his watch and saw it was time for the meeting. He needed to meet the men who ran this business before his company bought it.

He opened the door and stepped out into the bitter cold air. There was the smell of frost on the wind that made the late afternoon feel colder than it was. Already the sun headed toward the icy mountain peaks to the west.

Nathan walked confidently into the building. Gregory and Hal trailed behind him, dressed in dark suits and darker sunglasses. He liked both men, but he had enjoyed the freedom of Blue Aspen. He liked not having someone following him constantly.

The front entrance was made of glass and sparkled in the sunlight. Inside, a mural filled the entrance. There was a picture of a man with eighties-style hair and seventies-style mustache. He stood in front of a garage, the smile beaming from his handsome face.

Nathan studied the photo. He knew that smile. It was the same one he'd worn when he'd first started his company. The pride. The joy. The excitement for the future. He knew that look.

"That's George when he first started the company," a young man told Nathan. He wore a polo with the ECT logo. "If you'll follow me, the meeting room is this way."

Nathan followed the man to a large room. A conference table dominated the space, but the windows overlooked the mountains. It was a nice place for a meeting. He found the coffee maker on the side of the room and poured himself a cup.

The door opened and an older man walked in. He wore a nice suit, but he looked ragged. He'd tried to hide his balding hair by sweeping longer bits over the top. His eyes were sunken and defeat hung on his shoulders.

"George Element," the man said, holding out his hand. "Pleased to meet you."

This was George Element? The man in the photo was young and vibrant. This man should be in his early sixties, but looked like he was nearly eighty. His eyes were yellow and his skin like old parchment. He'd put on weight since the picture, and it didn't suit him.

Nathan wondered what had happened to George that had aged him so quickly.

"Thank you for meeting me here," Nathan replied. "You have a lovely campus."

George gave a small smile and he looked around, taking the place in. "That we do. Would you like a tour? I know you're moving the company to California, but you might as well see what you bought."

"Why not?" Nathan agreed. "We can talk as we walk."

George opened the glass doors to the conference room and headed out. "You're the one that came up with the Quad-Ram system, aren't you?"

"I am. It was my first big success."

"A real nice innovation," George agreed. "You still creating stuff like that?"

"Unfortunately, no." Nathan shook his head. "It's all meetings and business. You know the CEO life."

"That's disappointing. It was a reason we sold to you and not someone else. Because you innovate like we do." George shook his head slowly. He turned and faced Nathan, his eyes grim. "You're young. Don't let them do that to you."

"What do you mean?" Nathan asked, confused.

"I love computers. I love putting them together and figuring out ways to make them faster. I love figuring out how to make software more effective. How to make both of them work together better than before. That's why I made this company. That's what this company is supposed to do."

"That's why Paradigm bought you," Nathan said, not quite understanding what George was trying to say. "You're known for coming up with new tech."

George nodded. "Do you know why I'm selling Elements Computer Technologies?"

"I'm afraid I don't. I just know that we jumped at the chance to purchase it. You weren't struggling in the marketplace, so I assume it was for personal reasons?"

George tipped his head as a yes. "This company was my pride and joy." He reached out and touched the wall. "Until I lost why I started it. I got caught up in the money. I had to make more. I had to succeed *more*."

"That's not a bad thing," Nathan told him. That was the reason Nathan was CEO. Paradigm was successful, but it was the drive for more money and more success that drove him. Money was everything.

"I have more money than I know what to do with," George told him, focusing gray eyes on Nathan. "But it cost me. It cost me two marriages. It cost me seeing my kids grow up. I've never held my grandchildren. My own kids don't recognize me. Sure, I have a nice house. I drive a great car. But I'm not happy."

Nathan took a step back. For a moment, he could see himself in this man. The unhappiness. He hadn't done something he'd loved in years. He loved the money, but the building and designing was what made him happy. It didn't make him rich, though.

"I gave up my soul for money," George told him. "When I realized what it was doing to me, it was too late. So, I'm selling my company. I want to be happy. Money doesn't matter if no one loves you."

Nathan wasn't quite sure what to say to that. He simply nodded and followed the older man down a well lit hallway.

"I should be selling you on all the amazing things we've done," George said after a moment. "But instead I'm rattling my chains of regret at you. Don't mind me. I'm selling my life's work. I'm proud of ECT. The company is the best around. It's my decisions that I'm bitter about. I made my own decisions. I chose to be CEO. I chose to focus on the money. It's why ECT is so successful today."

Again, Nathan wasn't quite sure what to say to that. This was one of the stranger meetings he'd had for a while. He was wondering if maybe having the meeting here rather than California really was a good idea.

He looked over at George and did a double take. For a moment, he saw himself in twenty years. He saw someone who had chased the allure of money and had only money to show for it. A lonely existence. A ghost of the future possibilities of his life, carrying golden chains.

He shook himself and the vision vanished. It was probably the altitude making him see things. He probably just needed to hydrate better. He tossed his coffee into a trashcan and looked around at where they were.

"Wow. This is your view?" Nathan asked, eyes going wide. They stood on an upper walkway over what looked to be a cafeteria. Everything was made of glass and open to the amazing views all around. To the west, the mountains loomed into the sky. To the east, the plains stretched out for miles. The town stood directly in front of him. It was small and cheery. He could see the colorful lights of Christmas decorations starting to flutter on.

"This is everyone's favorite spot," George said with a proud smile. "That's Devonsville just down there."

"Is that the elementary school?" Nathan asked, picking out a large building with a flagpole. He wondered if Holly had received his gifts yet.

"It is," George replied. "We have one of the best school districts in the state. The Colorado State College is just a few miles north of here. They just ranked second in the nation for computer science programs. We work closely with the schools around here. It's easier to get the best talent before they know they're talent."

Nathan nodded, not really listening. His eyes were on the school. "Do you know Holly Jones?"

He felt dumb as soon as the words left his mouth. This was supposed to be a business meeting. He shouldn't be asking about a random school teacher.

"Jones... Jones..." George leaned against the railing and

thought for a moment. "I think she's a teacher at the school. I know her dad. He runs the bookstore in town. He also manages all our reference materials for us. Well, he did, anyway."

Nathan nodded. Paradigm would supply all the needed reference materials.

"Will you be here for Christmas?" George asked him.

"I'm not sure," Nathan replied. He was hoping to see Holly and convince her to come back to California with him. He loved the idea of seeing her in that swimsuit on a beach.

"If you are, we're having a parade on Friday. All the businesses make floats and the kids walk in it. It's great town spirit. And Jones throws a party on Christmas for the kids. Hands out presents. The whole town shows up. You should come if you're here."

"Thanks. I'll keep that in mind."

"Let me show you the rest of the place," George said, motioning them on. "I think you'll love our Research and Development area. It seems like something the creator of the quad-ram would appreciate."

<h1 style="text-align:center">CHAPTER 25</h1>

*M*erryweather

MERRYWEATHER CLOSED her eyes and smiled. The snow. The lights. The Christmas tree. It was all set up and perfect.

All that they needed was the kiss.

Merryweather rubbed her hands and made a little magic.

CHAPTER 26

*H*olly

HOLLY STEPPED out onto the street and watched as her breath frosted and drifted away. There was a boy in her class who claimed he was part dragon because he exhaled "smoke" whenever it was cold. She smiled, blowing out an extra long breath into the dark night.

Christmas was everywhere downtown. Holly wrapped her jacket around her and wandered the brightly lit streets. Window were filled with toys and goodies. Restaurants were filled with happy diners. Christmas lights sparkled everywhere.

Holly meandered down the street, pausing to look at the holiday themed windows of the stores. She made her way to the city center where the mayor made speeches and the holiday parade started and began. This year, the tree stood in the center of the courtyard. It was decorated in silver and purple with lights strung from top to bottom.

Carolers walked the streets wearing old fashioned clothes and singing in perfect harmony. Holly recognized several members of the group as the high school choir. She made sure to put a couple dollars in their tip jar.

"Thanks Ms. Jones," one of the singers piped up.

They paused and then began a beautiful rendition of Silent Night.

Holly stood with her eyes on the sparkling lights of the tree listening to the songs that made her remember her mother. Her mom hated this song. She would roll her eyes and complain that the baby Jesus would not have been silent, because babies are never silent.

And "sleep in heavenly peace" with a newborn? Her mother would just shake her head. And then sing the song in her soft voice. She always sang along with the Christmas carols.

Holly turned as the song ended.

And there was Nathan.

He stood watching her look at the tree with a smile on his face. He wore a long dark wool coat that fitted him perfectly. He took a step toward her and snow started to fall.

"Nathan?"

Holly walked toward him as if in a dream. It certainly felt dream like and perfect. His smile drew her to him like a magnet.

She kissed him. His lips were soft against hers. Gentle. His hands were warm as he cupped her face in them.

"Hi," she said, breathless and excited. Snowflakes danced and fell, landing on his dark hair and long eyelashes.

"Hi," he repeated. He leaned forward and kissed her again, as if he couldn't get enough of her taste. She knew that she most certainly couldn't get enough of his.

She reached over and felt his arm, squeezing up and down his bicep.

"Just making sure you are really here," she said.

"I'm real," he assured her. And he kissed her once more. She closed her eyes and lost herself to him for a moment.

"What are you doing here?" she asked when the kiss ended. Her eyes were big as she searched his face. "Not that I don't want you here. I do want you here. I just thought you were in California."

"I moved my meetings around," he replied nonchalantly. "I came to meet the company I just purchased. It seemed easier than flying them out to California. Besides, I promised someone I'd look into our plan of moving ECT."

Holly's heart filled to bursting. She hugged him, feeling the snow on his jacket press into her cheek.

She grinned up at him, finishing the hug. "I'm so glad you're here. I didn't think I'd see you again."

She suddenly remembered the generous donation to the school and the flowers.

"Did you get my text? I wanted to thank you for the 3D printers and the flowers," she said quickly. "I'm glad I can do it in person now."

"Did you like them?"

"Very much. The printers will be very loved. It was so generous of you."

He shrugged. "It's nothing," he assured her.

She caught his arm. "No, it's so much more. Thank you. It means the world to me."

His smile warmed her better than hot chocolate on a cold day. Those eyes made her body heat and when he looked at her, she couldn't help but smile.

"Have you eaten?" Nathan asked. White snowflakes stood out on the black wool of his jacket. "I was told that I have to try Devonsville Pub while I'm here. Apparently, they have the best burgers around."

"Did George Element tell you that?" Holly asked him.

"He did, actually," Nathan replied, looking surprised.

"He's a partial owner."

"Are there better burgers?"

"Nope. They're the best, but I figured you should know what you were getting into," Holly replied with a grin.

"So, you hungry?" He motioned down the road, a hopeful look on his face.

"Starving." She took his arm and together they walked down Main Street looking like they were ready to be photographed for a Christmas card. The snow was falling, the lights were twinkling, and they were walking arm in arm.

The restaurant was packed. Even on a Tuesday night, Devonsville Pub was the place to be. Nathan pulled open the heavy oak doors and they weaved their way around waiting patrons to put their name on the wait list.

"Two for dinner, please," Nathan told the hostess.

"It's an hour wait," she told him.

Nathan smiled disarmingly. "Are you sure you can't get us a table sooner?"

He reached into his pocket and pulled out his wallet. The young hostess just stared at him. "Still an hour, dude."

That's when Holly came up. "How long of a wait?" Holly asked.

"Oh, hi Ms. Jones," the hostess said with a grin. "He didn't say he was with you. Since you called ahead, we'll have your table ready in just a minute."

The hostess gave Holly a wink. Nathan looked over to see Holly smiling smugly at him. He didn't say anything with the press of people waiting around for a table. It was only a few minutes before the hostess had them seated at a small table near the back.

"You didn't call ahead, did you?" he asked Holly.

She picked up her menu and shook her head. "Nope."

"I'm a billionaire. I get the tables. She was going to make

me wait." Nathan shook his head in disbelief. "But you got us a table. How'd you do that?"

Holly grinned at him. "I don't know if you know this, but I'm kind of a local celebrity." She lowered the menu and her smiled grew smug. "I recently won this fancy educator's award. The town's pretty proud of me."

"See, I knew there were perks to dating you," Nathan said, picking up his menu and perusing it.

Holly's heart caught in her chest. Dating? Were they dating? She kept her menu upright, but peeked over the top, trying to see if he was acting nervous. Maybe he didn't mean to say that. Maybe he meant something else.

"Oh, the Colorado Burger sounds delicious," he said, her mouth scrunching slightly to the side. "Or maybe the Whiskey Burger..."

Holly settled back, hiding her face with the menu. She liked the idea of them dating. She liked the idea of anything to do with Nathan. She was still sure she was going to wake up at any moment and find out this was all just a dream.

He was here.

She wasn't about to look a gift horse in the mouth.

They ordered and Holly found it hard to eat. She was hungry and the food was delicious, but she couldn't seem to stop smiling long enough to put the food into her mouth. She was suddenly too excited to eat.

Nathan didn't seem to have that problem. He ate with gusto, enjoying every bite. They chatted and laughed. He asked her about her day and she about his. It felt so normal. So right. This was how the world was supposed to be, she could feel it.

For once, it felt like the universe was in tune and things were going well.

"Would you like a tour of Old Town?" Holly asked as they

finished their meal. She had most of her burger boxed up for later.

Nathan smiled at her. "I'd love one."

Together they walked out into the night. Snow fell softly, decorating the trees and lampposts with a coat of white. It was still early despite the December dark, so all the stores were still open. Holly showed him the store that sold crystals to fix your chakras, the antique market, and the high end pet food store.

"And here's my dad's bookstore," she said at the end of the tour. They stood outside the old brick building with snow still falling gently around them.

"He has some great sci-fi books in the front window," Nathan said, peering through the glass.

"Come on in and I'll buy you a cup of coffee." She pulled open the doors to the bookstore.

This was taking him to her special place. The bookstore was sacred. It was where she would hide from the world. Even though it was a store open to the public, it felt more like home than her apartment did.

She glanced back, nervously looking to see what Nathan thought of the place.

He stepped in, carefully brushing snow from his shoulders. He looked around and a slow smile filled his face.

"This is wonderful," he said, taking a step in. He went to a shelf of books, pulling one out and carefully looking it over. "This is such a good book."

He put his book back and found another. Holly watched him, loving that he was excited about books as she was. He darted around the bookshelves like a kid on Christmas morning.

"And you have the whole series? I can never find them," he exclaimed, caressing a bookshelf of titles. He looked up at her. "No wonder you wanted to stay here. I want to stay here."

She grinned. He loved books as much as she did.

"Let me buy you a cup of coffee," she said, guiding him over to the cafe portion. She ordered two cappuccinos and they took them to a small table off to the side of the bookstore. The cafe had a slow but steady stream of customers, but Holly and Nathan were far enough away that they were basically in their own little world.

"I would have loved this place as a kid," Nathan told her, settling in. He draped his jacket over the back of his chair, looking relaxed and like he belonged there.

"It was a great place to grow up," Holly agreed.

Nathan's eyes went distant. "My dad wouldn't have liked it," he said softly. "Not enough promise for a big payout."

"Sounds like a fun guy," Holly commented.

Nathan made a sound that could pass as a laugh, but was utterly mirthless. "He wasn't a bad man. He just didn't know what to do with a child. He had these ideas, but never the plan to accomplish them. He always said it was the lack of funding, but it was more than that."

Holly sipped at her coffee, wrapping her fingers around the warm mug. She watched as Nathan's kind eyes filled with long-lost hurt.

"Do you see him around Christmas?" Holly asked.

Nathan shook his head. "No. We aren't really close. He was never big on Christmas anyway. It was more important to work."

"I'm sorry," she told him.

He shook himself, flinging away his bad memories as if they were water droplets off a dog. "It's something I've learned to deal with. Now, tell me more about this parade on Friday. I'm told it's something the whole town participates in?"

Holly let him change the subject. "So, the kids and local business all show up. There's candy and floats and music. The high school marching band does a special performance every year, right outside the Mayor's office. It's how I know Christmas is really here. Will you be here?"

"I should be," he told her. Holly felt her stomach zing with hope.

"Really?"

He nodded, sipping at his coffee. "I have lots of meetings tomorrow. I'm helping to inspect the building and see what assets we can salvage. Thursday, is more of the same. I need to go back to California Friday night."

"You mean you have to leave before Christmas?" Holly was surprised by the amount of disappointment in her voice.

"I have work to do," he told her gently.

"Right." She nodded. "I remember."

Nathan asked her about the parade again, and she tried not to think about his leaving. He just felt so right here. She didn't want him to leave. She felt greedy wanting more of him, yet she couldn't help it.

She began to wonder if maybe there was a way to use the magic of the parade and the holiday to convince him to stay. She certainly felt like there was enough magic in Christmas that it could happen.

CHAPTER 27

Nathan

NATHAN COULD HARDLY BELIEVE how easy and wonderful it was to talk with Holly. He remembered it being good while they were at the ski resort, but this was so much better. Surrounded by books and sipping on coffee, he felt like they could talk about everything.

And they did.

They had close enough opinions on politics that they didn't argue, but could hold a lively debate. Neither one of them had much time for television, but the few shows they did watch they shared their enjoyment. She got up several times to show him a book he hadn't heard of or to find one that he recommended.

It was a perfect evening.

"Closing time," a man's voice called from across the store. It was then that Nathan noticed the lights had dimmed and the low chatter of customers had faded. Even the sound of the coffee maker was gone. He looked over to see the cafe dark and everything cleaned.

"Sorry, Dad," Holly said, standing up and kissing the man on the cheek. "I guess we lost track of time."

The man had Holly's hair color and eyebrow shape. He was clearly Holly's father, the owner of the store.

"Mark Jones," the man said, holding out a hand to Nathan. "Nathan Reed."

A slight widening of the eyes and a glance over at his daughter were the only indications that Mark knew who Nathan was. Mark looked back and forth between Nathan and his daughter, his face unreadable.

"Well, it's a pleasure to meet you Nathan," Mark told him. "But, I'm afraid I need you to get out of my store. We've been closed for over an hour."

"My apologies," Nathan said quickly.

"Dad, you realize you're kicking me out with a man, right?" Holly put a hand to her hip.

"When you put it that way..." Mark scratched his head. "I think you're grown enough to make good decisions. Lord knows you do things your own way regardless of what I tell you to do. Maybe if I tell you to go off with him you'll do just the opposite."

A quick stab of worry flickered through Nathan. He really hoped Holly wouldn't do that.

Instead she just shook her head and picked up her jacket. "We'll go find another coffee shop. Alley Cat Coffee is open until the bars close. We can go there."

Mark smiled at his daughter as she kissed his cheek one last time.

"Nathan." Mark's tone was friendly, but still a warning to be good to his daughter. Nathan had no doubt that this father would come after him if he did anything to hurt Holly.

"Good night, Dad," Holly said with a smile, grabbing

Nathan's hand and pulling him to the back door. "I'll see you tomorrow."

"Good night, sir," Nathan said respectfully before Holly pulled him through the door. He could see Mark smiling and shaking his head as he finished closing up his store.

"So, that's my dad," Holly said as they stumbled out into the alley. The snow had stopped, but it was colder now. Nathan checked his watch to see it was just after eleven.

"I like him," Nathan told her honestly.

Holly chuckled. "I think everyone does," she told him. "If you want to get on his good side, start talking to him about Ian Fleming's books versus the James Bond movies."

"I'll keep that in mind," Nathan said, storing away the tip for future use. "Does he like the movies or the books better?"

Holly turned and gave him a look that said it should be obvious. The man did own a bookstore after all.

She stopped where the alley joined to a bigger street. Many of the shops had turned off their lights and closed up for the night. The Christmas lights still sparkled and twinkled in the windows, but everything else was dark. She looked up at him, chewing on her bottom lip.

"You don't want to go to the coffee shop, do you?" he asked her, a smile forming on his face. She shook her head and smiled at him.

"We can go to my place, but just know that it's tiny. And messy. I wasn't exactly expecting guests, and I haven't actually finished unpacking from the ski trip," she admitted.

"So my hotel?" he offered. "It's a hotel room, but it is clean."

She laughed, taking his hand. "Do you want to drive or should I?"

❄

HOLLY DROVE. Nathan was surprised that her ancient car could move at all, but somehow it started and the heat even worked. It was definitely a different experience than driving in his Porsche. The streets were quiet other than an occasional snowplow, so he didn't mind driving in the older car.

Nathan could see Hal in the dark SUV behind them gnashing his teeth about it, but Nathan had wanted to ride with Holly. She needed to have her car so she could make it in to work tomorrow morning. Hal suggested they could take two cars, but Nathan didn't want to be separated from her for that long.

Holly parked her car in the parking lot and together they headed up to his room. The lobby was quiet other than a bored looking man at the front desk. He barely acknowledged the two of them coming in with hands held. He didn't even blink when Hal followed them in, all hulking muscles and scary looks.

Nathan figured the man probably saw it all at the night shift desk at a hotel like this one.

Nathan pressed the button for the elevator. Holly's hair glistened with snow and her cheeks were red from the cold. She kept looking over at him and smiling.

That smile made his world spin. She was beautiful, inside and out. When she grinned at him like that, he felt like the luckiest man in the world.

His body started to think of her grinning at him like that without clothes on. The elevator seemed to take forever. Finally, the machine dinged and the metal doors slid open.

He and Holly stepped inside. Hal moved to follow them, but he held up his hand.

"This one's full. Get the next one." Nathan tapped the door-close button and ignored Hal's unhappy look. He'd hear about this later from Gregory, but for right now, he just wanted to be alone in the elevator with Holly.

With the doors closed, they were alone. Holly turned and kissed him just as he turned and reached for her. She moaned softly as their mouths met, turning up the flame in Nathan's belly.

He pressed her into the wall, using his body to put her where he wanted. She was so warm and perfect pressed up against him. She still tasted of coffee. His hands roamed under her jacket and she arched her back to offer herself up to him.

He nearly ripped her shirt off right there in the elevator. It was that tempting.

It was only the doors opening and the soft ding that kept him under control. The door to his room was just around the corner. He could be control his urges and his need to feel her skin under his for the twenty steps it took to get to the door.

That was, until she bit her lip.

The lip bite with the big green eyes and the mussed hair was too much. He couldn't stop himself. He had to kiss her again, this time with tongue and teeth. She groaned softly as they stumbled down the hallway, trying to walk but trying to make out at the same time.

He pressed her body against the door, kissing her while he blindly searched his pockets for his key. Finally, he found it, stabbing it into the door.

The door opened, and together they tumbled into his bedroom.

*N*athan

"You want to come to school with me today?"

Nathan lay naked in bed, his body exhausted but mind serene. Holly stood in the light of the bathroom brushing her hair. She wore the same pants as the night before, but she'd pulled out a clean sweater from the backseat of her car. It was good enough that it made it look like she'd gone home and changed.

He loved watching her. She moved with careful grace as she checked her face in the mirror.

"Did you hear me?" she asked again, coming to the bed with a smile on her face. "Do you want to come to school with me today?"

He reached out and traced a finger along her cheek. "I have meetings this morning. What about lunch?"

She thought about it for a moment and then leaned over

and kissed his forehead. "I'll save you a seat at the cool kids' table."

He chuckled, watching as she picked up her bag and slid into her boots. She gave him one last smile before disappearing out the door and into the early morning.

The room felt empty without her. When he'd checked in, the room had felt tiny. It was smaller than what he was used to. Now that Holly had left, the room felt much too large. He wished she were back in the soft bed with him, her hair falling across her face as she snuggled with him.

He was falling for her. He knew it deep in his soul. She was perfect for him. The fact that he'd found her at all was sheer luck. It felt like some kind of magic that they'd managed to cross paths time and time again.

A sigh escaped him as he leaned back, spread eagle on the bed. What was his plan here? He wasn't sure. His job was in California, and he didn't want to do a long distance thing. He could afford the plane trips, but his schedule wouldn't. Lucy was already chiding him for the missed meetings at home. He was behind.

Nathan ran a hand across his face. He needed to think. He needed to focus and come up with a plan. He thought about putting on his gym clothes and utilizing the gym on the second floor, but that didn't seem like enough. He needed something for his brain more than his mind today.

So he put on his clothes and told Hal to get the car. They were going to Elements Computer Technologies Campus. Hal drove while Nathan made phone calls and answered emails.

The campus was quiet when Nathan arrived. With the upcoming holidays and the company moving to California, many employees had taken leave. Nathan could feel the uncertainty hanging in the air as he walked around. Many employees were debating if the move was worth it, and if they'd even have a job in a year if they did move.

Nathan passed the photo of young George without looking at it. He walked quickly and with a purpose down the hallway and to the left. He already knew which corridor to turn down and he had his access card ready before he hit the door.

The innovation area. It was for research and development and testing out new ideas. If Nathan had to start all over again, this is where he would begin. This was where he loved to work.

The department was empty. Nathan wandered around until he found a mostly empty desk. He sat down and stretched out his legs. Soft winter sunlight filled the small room. There were rows of computer parts along the back wall along with various tools. Nathan opened up his own desk and found it full of mismatched tools. There were pliers, screwdrivers, wire crimpers, spudger and pry bars, and more.

It reminded him of his work space when he first started years ago.

He started when the door beeped and swung open. A young man in casual clothes sauntered in, a thin black laptop under his arm. He dropped the laptop on Nathan's desk.

"Oh, hey. I have this laptop. It's busted," the man explained. "My supervisor said to bring it to you guys since you always need parts and stuff."

"Thanks." Nathan decided not to reveal that he was actually the big boss. No need to freak the guy out. Everyone he'd met here so far had been kind and friendly.

The man waved his hand and exited the door, leaving Nathan alone with the busted laptop.

Nathan looked at it for a moment and then picked it up. He inspected the casing and the power inputs. He tried turning it on. The laptop was definitely busted. He rolled up his sleeves and went to work.

Nathan's hands knew what to do. He opened the casing and pulled the computer apart. His hands found the tools he needed and his fingers remembered how to use them. Fixing the laptop barely took any conscious effort.

It felt good.

Ideas started to come to him. He could make the laptop slimmer by reducing the fan size. Tweaking the ports would allow more efficient use of the wiring.

He was transported back in time to when he was just starting out. He used to do this under a single light bulb in a storage rental. It was there that he'd created the Quad-ram. He'd been the first to come up with it, and now it was standard. He had his fingerprints on nearly every computer in the world, simply because he'd tinkered while fixing another computer.

It was easier to think back then. There were less complications. Nathan reached for a pair of pliers, bending a piece back into place.

What if he stayed here? What if he didn't move Elements Computer Technologies to California? The campus was set up and running. They had some of the best talent flowing in by way of the college. The town supported them.

And that would mean that he had a legitimate reason to stay out here as well.

The possibility tugged at him.

He shook his head. It would cost too much. It wouldn't work. The board wouldn't go for it. There were a million reasons, most of them dollars, that it wouldn't work. He pushed the idea away. He would lose money doing that, and money was what mattered.

"There," Nathan said, putting the laptop back together. He

plugged it in and the screen flickered to life. Nathan sat back, admiring his work. Pride filled him, rushing and heady.

He played around on the laptop, making sure it really was fixed. He liked the idea of leaving ECT where it was. He'd look into what the cost would be. He worried that he would lose money, but for the first time in a long time, it didn't eat at his soul.

He shut down the laptop and carefully set it up on a shelf. He looked around, hoping for another busted computer that he could fix. He liked fixing. His mind was able to find solutions not only to the repair, but also to his business.

He should have done this for RentTech. He'd botched that addition to the company. He was surprised the board hadn't fired him on the spot. Millions of dollars lost because of him. He'd made the wrong choice. It was all fixed now, but he still felt the sting of near failure.

He'd lost money because of it.

He found another discarded computer. This one was a desktop model, probably a couple years old. He already started making mental checklists of things to do: new memory, a new processor, check the wiring...

And then it dawned on him. It was estimated he earned around one hundred thousand dollars an hour at the minimum. He'd spent an hour putting this laptop back together.

This was the world's most expensive laptop. And it wasn't even that good.

He set the desktop back down and took a step back.

His phone beeped. It was time for his meeting.

Nathan groaned. He wanted to stay and fix the worthless computer. He hated these meetings. He hated the financial speak and the smarmy handshakes. It was as far from fixing and creating things as he could get.

Yet, it paid well.

And money was what was important. Money was everything.

He sighed and straightened the sleeves on his shirt. He glanced over at the now working laptop one last time before leaving the room and turning out the lights.

It was time to get to work.

CHAPTER 29

*H*olly

HOLLY CHECKED her watch for the millionth time that day. She wanted it to be lunch time. She wasn't even all that hungry. She just wanted to see Nathan. She wanted to show him where she worked and what she did all day. She wanted to share her world with him.

The morning dragged on. Even her students said that it felt like lunch was taking forever. They complained more than usual and no one wanted to stay in their own seats. It made for a very long morning.

I'M BRINGING LUNCH.

HOLLY READ the message from Nathan and grinned. The cafeteria food was decent, especially since today was tacos, but it was mass produced and geared toward children. She tried to bring her lunch as often as possible, but she still ended up eating chicken nuggets or macaroni and cheese at least once a week.

"Ten more minutes, and then it's lunch time," Holly called out to her class. "Please finish up the math worksheets and clean up your math blocks."

She was answered by the sound of blocks falling and scattering all over the floor. One of her students looked up at her with big eyes and an empty bucket. The blocks littered the floor by his feet. Holly sighed and motioned for him to start picking up.

The kids were restless. They needed to eat and go out and burn off some of their energy. It was the second to last day of school before break, and the kids were ready to be out.

Only one more day and then they'd all be free for a couple of weeks. Even though Holly adored teaching, she was excited for the break. Sleeping in and eating things that weren't chicken nuggets sounded wonderful.

The kids were busy putting things away and preparing for lunch when the principal walked in.

"Hello, Mr. Sheppard," the kids chorused as soon as they saw him. He was a big man with kind eyes and no hair on his head. He reminded Holly of a magic genie, if genies went into education.

"Ms. Jones," Mr. Sheppard said, his face stern and hard. "You and your class need to go to the cafeteria right now."

Holly frowned. The look on Mr. Sheppard's face was unhappy and that meant whatever happened next was not going to be good. This was the face reserved for troublemakers and suspensions. This was the face he used when there was bad news.

Holly swallowed hard and herded her kids into a line. They all moved quickly and quietly, seeing the look on Mr.

Sheppard's face. Several of the kids whispered quietly, falling silent whenever Mr. Sheppard turned to look at them.

They walked down the hallways with Holly's heart rate speeding up with every step. Was she having her award taken away? Was there an emergency? Was her father okay? Was this about the extra glitter she'd spilled on the floor last week making posters?

Mr. Sheppard crossed his arms and stood in front of the double doors leading into the cafeteria.

"Ms. Jones." His low voice was dangerous. Holly hurried up quickly from the back of the line. "You go in first."

Holly swallowed hard, unsure of what was going to happen. She pushed open the doors and was greeted by the scent of pizza. And not school pizza, but real pizzeria pizza.

Standing in the center of the cafeteria was Nathan. Behind him, dozens of boxes of pizza stood waiting for hungry children to come eat them.

Mr. Sheppard clapped a hand on her shoulder, laughter spilling out of him. 'You should see your face," he told her. "I'm sorry. I couldn't help it."

Holly looked around, slow on the uptake.

"I brought lunch," Nathan explained, coming to greet her. "I just brought enough for the whole school."

"You brought pizza for the whole school?" Holly asked, looking around. The kids started streaming in through the doors, cheering with excitement and rushing for the boxes.

Mr. Sheppard shook Nathan's hand. "Thank you for sponsoring this."

"It's my pleasure," Nathan told him. "I have to make my end of the year donations somehow, right?"

Mr. Sheppard laughed and went to help guide some lost kindergartners to the pizza.

Holly went over and kissed Nathan on the cheek. She

didn't want to do more in front of her students, but Nathan blushed like she'd frenched him.

"Thank you," she told him.

"Did I ever tell you my favorite teacher was in second grade?" he asked her. She shook her head and he leaned in close. "I like you better, though."

She chuckled and grinned. "You get me cheese pizza?"

Nathan reached around and held out a box. He popped open the lid to reveal a beautiful cheese pizza. Her mouth watered.

"I have plates at a table." He looked over behind him and shrugged. "Well, I had plates. It looks like some fifth graders swiped them."

He chuckled and they found an open space to sit down. The room was full of cheerful kids. Everyone was excited about the free pizza. Nathan had even ordered a couple gluten free pies and some without dairy to include the kids on diet restrictions.

Holly picked a slice up out of the box and ate it without a plate. Nathan grinned and copied her. They sat on long benches that were made for children rather than adults.

"Ms. Jones, can we sit with you?" Molly North asked her. A girl and a boy stood behind her, all of them holding plates full of pizza and looking hopeful.

"Of course you can," Holly said. "Come sit with us. I'd like you to meet my friend, Nathan. He's the one who brought the pizza today."

"You brought all this pizza?" Jake Bennet asked, his dark eyes going wide. "That musta cost, like, a million dollars."

"It wasn't a million dollars," Nathan told the boy. "But, what if it was? What if I got enough pizza to fill this entire cafeteria?"

"We'd have to swim in it," Natasha Aldovi replied. She

took a big bite of her pizza and looked thoughtful. "Would a life jacket work in pizza?"

"Probably not," Nathan answered. "But it might work in Jello. Maybe we could fill the cafeteria with jello."

The three kids giggled and they started calling out foods that they could fill the cafeteria with, each one becoming more outrageous than the last. Nathan was right there with them, coming up with ridiculous ideas and spurring them on.

In essence, Holly was sitting with four second graders. She loved it.

"Chocolate chips," Nathan told the girl sitting next to him as he munched on a piece of pizza. "Then we could make cookie ships."

"I like to make chocolate chip cookies for Santa," Natasha answered. "Do you like chocolate chip cookies?"

"I do," Nathan said, nodding his head.

Natasha's eyes narrowed and she looked him over. "Are you secretly Santa?"

Nathan's eyes went wide and he choked a little on his pizza. "No, I am most definitely not Santa. Why would you think that?"

"Because you like chocolate chip cookies and you brought us all a present. And you brought Ms. Jones a present too," Natasha explained. "I gotta make sure of these things."

Nathan tapped on his chest, still recovering from inhaling pizza. "That's a good thing to do."

Holly couldn't stop herself from laughing.

Soon the pizza was gone and the kids headed out to the playground. Holly helped the kids pick up their plates and empty boxes, getting them into the trash cans.

"I'm on playground duty today," she told him. "You're welcome to stay if you want."

Holly bit her lower lip, hoping that he would. She didn't

want him to leave. Ever. Having him at school was combining two of her favorite things together and she found she was enjoying it immensely.

"Mr. Nathan, sir," Jake said, appearing out of nowhere and tugging on Nathan's shirt. "Will you come play with us?"

"You know what? I haven't been on a playground in ages," he said to Jake. "I think I need to change that."

Nathan flashed Holly a grin. Jake's small hand wrapped around Nathan's and the boy pulled him out of the cafeteria and out onto the playground. Holly followed, chuckling behind them.

Sunshine filled the playground. The snow had mostly melted, leaving random puddles of cold wet surprises at the bottom of the slides and in soggy patches of the fields. The children all wore their winter coats and mashed hats onto their heads. Random gloves lay scattered like fallen soldiers near the door, casualties of not being put on fast enough.

Nathan ran out to the playground and the children quickly called him into a game of Groundies. Six children tried to explain the rules to him, all of them jumping around from rule to rule without rhyme or reason.

"Help?" Nathan asked as Holly came over.

"It's a combo of Marco Polo and tag. The 'it' person has to have their eyes closed while they are on the playground equipment. You can open your eyes on the ground," Holly explained.

Nathan looked at the slide and plastic bridge. "Wouldn't it be safer to have your eyes open on the equipment and closed on the ground?"

"Yes, but way less fun," Holly agreed. "If the not-it players touch the ground, the it player can call out 'Groundies" and if the not-it player is still on the ground, they become it."

Nathan looked over at the kids. "I'm guessing I'm it."

All the kids' heads nodded in unison.

Nathan jumped up the ladder and screwed his eyes shut. "Okay. I'm coming for you!"

The kids shrieked with delight and scattered across the play-structure. Nathan played like he was seven years old, except that he was happy to be it and chase the kids around.

The kids adored him. She knew that several of them knew who he was, yet they welcomed him. They didn't ask him about their parent's jobs. They just accepted him since he brought pizza.

Holly watched with a smile on her face. Nathan was good with the kids. They loved playing with him. He seemed to love playing in return. Over the course of the recess, she watched him lose the stress around his eyes. He laughed. He ran.

And she realized she was in love.

CHAPTER 30

*N*athan

NATHAN HADN'T HAD a workout like that in months. When the whistle finally blew signifying the end of their time outside, he was drenched in sweat and his legs were shaking.

The kids seemed unfazed.

"How do they have so much energy?" Nathan asked Holly as they followed the classroom back inside.

"They weren't picking each other up and swinging them in circles," Holly reminded him. She smiled when she said it, her voice warm and soft.

"Okay, friends. Put your coats away and we'll head to art class." The kids continued shouting and talking, but they did as she asked, hanging up their coats on the pegs along the far side of the classroom.

Once the coats were put away, they formed a rough semblance of a line.

"I'm just going to take them to art class," Holly told him. "It'll only take a minute."

"I'll wait here. I don't have to be back just yet."

A smile filled her face and then she darted around, making sure that the kids were ready. As soon as the door opened, the kids became quiet as they walked through the halls.

Ms. Jones runs a tight ship, Nathan thought to himself. The kids obviously loved her. To be honest, he loved her too. She had the ability to make someone feel like they were special and mattered in the world. It was a gift.

Nathan looked around the small classroom. There were about thirty small desks with tiny chairs for the tiny people to sit and learn. Holly had a regular sized government issued desk in the corner. It was stacked high with papers and projects and the flowers he'd gotten her.

The walls were brick, but Holly had made them warm and inviting. She had posters up with book covers and funny math jokes. Lining the room were handmade snowflakes in all different shapes and designs.

Nathan realized there were words written on each snowflake. He went over and read one.

I wish that I didn't have to move. I wish that Dad's didn't have to go to California.

Also, I wish for a puppy that doesn't make me sneeze.

The innocence of the wish hit him like a hard punch to the gut. He read the next snowflake.

I WISH *my mom didn't have to worry about her job. I wish that she could be happy again.*

Also, I wish for a unicorn.

THAT ONE WAS MARKED with Molly's name.

I WISH FOR WORLD PEACE. *I wish there were no more bad guys.*

Also, I wish for a brother.

NATHAN WAS STARTING to see the pattern. Three wishes.

I WISH *my sister didn't bite so much. I wish I had a dog.*

Also, I wish for a new sled.

I WISH *my parents didn't fight about moving. I don't want a new house.*

Also, I don't want socks this year.

THE MORE SNOWFLAKES HE READ, the more he saw the wishes echo one another. The kids didn't want to move. They liked their town. They liked their homes.

He couldn't blame them. He liked it here too.

I WISH *that Dad's company hadn't been bought. I wish I could buy it so we could stay here.*

Also, I wish for more Legos.

THE THOUGHT from earlier popped into his head. What if he stopped the move? What if he kept ECT here?

Would it really be that expensive? How much would he really lose?

And, the question that shocked him the most, did he even care that it would cost him money?

Nathan stared at the snowflakes. He read and reread the messy handwriting. He knew what each child he'd met today wanted for Christmas or whatever holiday they celebrated at home.

For the first time, the consequences of moving the company had faces. He wasn't just making money. He was changing these kids' lives. And for what?

Money.

Because money was what mattered.

Nathan could hear his father voice repeat the mantra in his head. *Money is what matters. Money is what matters.*

He wasn't sure that it was the only thing that mattered, though.

He needed more information. He called Lucy.

"What's up boss-man?" the familiar voice asked after the first ring. "You ready to come home yet?"

"No, actually. I want you to send me the financials on ECT."

"Which ones?" Lucy asked. He could hear her typing in the background.

"All of them. I want to see if it really is the best option to move this company to California. They have a lot of things going for them here that we can't replicate," Nathan explained.

"Boss, I don't think that's a good idea," Lucy said.

"I didn't ask you if it was a good idea. I'm the CEO. It's my call."

Lucy was quiet for a moment on the other end of the line. "Fine. I'll get them to you by the end of the hour."

And she hung up on him.

Nathan ran his hand through his hair. Now that he'd said something out loud, he wasn't sure if he was crazy or brilliant.

He'd just have to check the numbers. The numbers would tell him what to do. Money was what mattered.

"Sorry that took so long," Holly said, coming back into the classroom. "A couple of teachers caught me in the hall. They all want to thank you for the pizza."

Seeing Holly made his worries grow distant. She looked beautiful. She wore dark slacks with a soft gray wool sweater. Her dirty-blonde hair hung in a messy ponytail with strands softening her face. She looked like a model.

"You're looking at me like you might still be hungry," Holly teased him.

"Maybe I'm just hot for teacher," he replied. He took a step into her, his leg going between hers and his hands on her waist.

She shivered with desire and looked up at him with big eyes.

And then his phone rang, breaking the mood.

She stepped back, her face flushed as she looked around, glancing out the open door to the empty hallway. She grinned at him, though, telling him that she'd liked it.

"I have to go back to ECT," he told her, putting his phone back in his pocket. "But, can I buy you dinner later?"

"I'd like that," she told him. She did one more glance at the door before going up on her toes and kissing him on the mouth. Her tongue touched his for the briefest of moments before she pulled back and smiled at him.

"I'll see you at five, Ms. Jones." His whole body tingled from her kiss.

It was going to be a rough couple of hours to get through with that sexy of a kiss on his mind. But, he glanced back to see her eyes on him, it would be worth the wait.

CHAPTER 31

*M*erryweather

THIS WAS her favorite part of the magic. This was the part that was effortless. It was also the most dangerous part of love magic.

This was where it was easy to become complacent. To lose focus. Things were easy, but that didn't mean they were set in stone.

Merryweather knew this. She needed to stay vigilant if she was going to make this love story work, because somehow, she knew that it was never as easy as it should be.

Nathan

SOMEONE WAS KNOCKING on his door.

Holly had already left for the morning. She wore jeans and a dark green sweater with a sparkly reindeer on it. She looked hot, even if the sweater was ridiculous. But then, Nathan suspected he would find anything Holly wore to be attractive.

He opened the door expecting to see Hal or maybe someone from the hotel. Instead, it was Lucy.

She stood, looked annoyed as hell in a dark red pencil skirt and matching jacket. Her jet black hair was pulled back and away from her face. Her dark gray eyes were focused directly on him.

Despite being her boss, when she looked at him like that, he didn't feel like he was the one in control.

"Hey Boss. Surprise."

"Lucy, it's good to see you. Come on in." Nathan held the

door open for her. He was glad he was dressed and the living room of the hotel suite was cleaned up.

Lucy looked around and sniffed. "This is where you're staying?"

Nathan looked around. He'd gotten used to the small room. It wasn't nearly as nice as his house or the Ritz, but it was comfortable for what he needed. Plus, Gregory said the staff was amazing and were doing everything he asked.

The entire town seemed to be full of helpful, welcoming people. The woman at the front desk always greeted him with a smile. The coffee-stand lady gave him extra coffee for free. He was beginning to feel like he belonged here.

"What are you doing here, Lucy?" Nathan asked. He leaned against the wall, his arms crossed.

"I'm here to help," she replied. "You said you're thinking of canceling the move, so I came out to assist. Since I've been the one setting everything up, I'll know what to do."

Her words chafed him a little bit. He should have been the one setting everything up, but he'd handed it off to Lucy because it was the part of the job he didn't like. It was his own fault that things were the way they were.

"Thanks for coming to help, Lucy," Nathan said, softening his tone. Lucy wasn't the enemy here. If anything, she would know what to do. She was an asset. That's why he hired her in the first place.

"I'm here to make Paradigm money," she said with a smile. "If that means I come out to middle of nowhere to do it, I do."

"Are you staying at this hotel?" Nathan asked.

"God, no." Lucy made a sour face. "I found a hotel downtown. There's no way I would stay in a place like this. No offense, Nathan, but this is Podunk."

Nathan looked at her very sleek and very expensive designer suit. It clashed with the carpet and walls of the hotel. This was a nice hotel by most people's standards, but it wasn't exactly billionaire level quality.

"I'll tell Hal to get the car," Nathan said. He punched the code into his phone and messaged Hal. Then, he put his jacket on as he left the room, heading across the hallway. He would meet Hal in the lobby.

The soft clink of silverware and soft breakfast chatter drifted in from the restaurant attached to the lobby. Nathan thought about picking up a cup of coffee, but the coffee at the Elements would be better. He could wait. Lucy followed him down and they headed out to the car.

Hal had the sleek SUV ready in the entrance. Nathan held the door open for Lucy to slide in across the leather seats. He followed her into the warm cabin of the car and Hal pulled the car away from the curb.

Lucy pulled out her tablet, put on her glasses, and began going over his schedule for the day. Nathan could feel his enthusiasm for the day fading away. There were so many meetings. There was no way for him to escape off to the R&D area and tinker with a computer again.

"You okay?" Lucy asked, peeking at him from over her stylish frames.

"I'm fine," he lied. He felt irritable and grumpy. The past few days, he'd felt free. With Lucy here, he could feel his job trapping him again. He didn't want to go to meetings. He had an idea on how to upgrade the laptop in the R&D department

Lucy frowned. She tapped on her tablet and her frown deepened.

"What?" Nathan asked her.

Lucy paused. "I thought telling you your money might cheer you up." She twisted her mouth. "But you're not going to like it today."

"How bad is it?"

"Just a little," she said. "And it's just due to some stocks. Market fluctuation. It'll be fine."

"Which stocks?"

Lucy's mouth thinned. "Paradigm's. News of RentTech's issues got out," she explained. "Investors are wary, especially with the holidays and the recent of acquisitions of two more similar companies."

"How much?"

Lucy wavered, checking the balance on the pad again. "Thirty mil."

Outwardly, Nathan didn't change his expression. Outwardly, he simply nodded, his face unreadable and expressionless.

Inwardly, he cringed. Could nothing go right with Rent-Tech? It wasn't even his responsibility anymore and it still haunted him. And thirty million dollars down? He felt like he'd been slapped. Granted, he'd lost that much and more on bad stock market days, but it never felt good. It didn't give him the thrill that seeing it up did. Losing money always put him in a bad mood.

He turned and stared out the window at the gray landscape. It matched his mood. Meetings all day with no reprieve. It was going to be a long day.

They drove in silence the rest of the way to the ECT campus.

Hal stopped the car and hurried around, opening the door for Nathan to get out. The cold wind bit at Nathan's nose and ears. He only had a suit jacket on for the short walk from the car to the building. He helped Lucy out of the car, and together they hustled into the warmth of the building.

"Ugh. I don't like the cold," Lucy announced once they were inside. "Give me that California sun every day of the week." She shivered and rubbed her arms. "I can't believe you willingly go out in snow."

Nathan chuckled. "It's fun once you get used to it."

Lucy made a face and shivered again. "No, thank you."

She looked around the lobby of the building. Lucy looked out of place here. Here dark red clothes contrasted sharply with the pale blues and light colors of the office. Her sharp elegant look was jarring against the comfortable calming tone of the office.

"Your first meeting is in the Elbert Room," Lucy said, reading off her tablet. "You ready?"

Nathan sighed. He looked wistfully toward the R&D department, but knew that he couldn't go there today. He couldn't play with the laptop. He couldn't install the new driver he wanted to test. He couldn't play with a RAM configuration that was teasing his brain with possibilities.

No. He had to go to endless meetings.

He sighed again, resigning himself to his fate. At least the view out the windows was better here.

The meetings dragged all day.

They were tedious.

They were boring.

It was awful.

This was the part of the job that he loathed, yet it seemed to be the part that took up most of his time. He had to placate different groups. There were conference calls and egos to be soothed. He had to come up with solutions for problems that didn't even exist yet.

There were some upsides to the meetings today. He learned about how well this office worked here. His plan to keep ECT in Colorado, rather than moving it and the employees to California was sounding better and better.

There were families here. There were mentorships and history. The company thrived here. Plus, he got to meet some of the new graduates from the computer science program at the local college. They were good. They were really good, and since they weren't from Silicon Valley, they weren't nearly as expensive.

The more meetings he went to, the more convinced he became that the move to California was a bad idea. He knew that the company had already invested money in the move, but he could eat that cost. It would still be cheaper than packing up everything.

Unfortunately, Lucy disagreed.

The two of them sat at lunch. Everyone else sat apart, as if they had some contagious disease. He sat and ate his turkey sandwich, trying not to count the hours until dinner. Dinner was with Holly and would be his bright spot for the entire day.

Lucy reached across the table and took one of his chips. He glared at her, but she just smiled at him, popping the chip into her mouth.

"You doing okay?" she asked him, swiping another chip from his plate.

"I will be if you stop stealing my food," he replied, playfully moving his plate away from her. She grinned, trying again. This time he blocked her with his fork.

"There, there's that smile," she said, pointing to his face. "I haven't seen it all day."

Nathan rolled his eyes, but pushed his plate toward her. "Have as many chips as you want."

She grinned at him. "Thanks." She reached across and took two this time. "So, I wanted to talk to you about moving ECT to California."

"I don't think we should do it," he told her. "This place is good for the company. If we move them, we risk losing what made them a good acquisition in the first place."

Lucy crunched thoughtfully for a moment. "And your decision has nothing to do with a pretty blonde that happens to live just down the road?"

"No."

Lucy raised her eyebrows and reached for another chip. "I think you need to reevaluate that statement."

"There is a woman that I find attractive in this town. Does that mean that I would risk an entire business on my lust? No. I think ECT should stay in Devonsville because it's the best place for ECT."

Lucy sighed and pushed away her own plate. "I was afraid of this," she said, shaking her head. "You aren't thinking this through. Yes, this place is great. There are some perks here. But they aren't good enough to stop the move."

Nathan crossed his arms and looked at Lucy. "Why?"

"The tax break. Moving a small business gets us a lot of great tax opportunities. We're talking millions. And, it's good for our image," Lucy explained. "I can give you the exact numbers if you want, but the money making move is to go to California."

Nathan shook his head. "Short term, maybe," he conceded. "But, long term, staying here is the better option. Yes, we won't make as much money this year, but the potential for more profit is here."

"Nathan, I'm not going to argue this with you." Lucy carefully stacked up her empty plates. "I'm telling you that you're blinded by this girl and the novelty of this town. I'm not trying to be mean."

"I know, Lucy." Nathan sighed. He still felt in his bones that his was the right decision. He knew it just like he knew how to reprogram a buggy device. It felt right. It made sense to him.

"Look, I know you. You're going to think about it for the rest of the day. You're going to research it and you'll realize what I'm telling you is right," Lucy told him. "Please don't repeat RentTech."

Nathan looked up at her. He had followed his gut on

RentTech. He had done what he thought was best. And it had blown up in his face. RentTech was operating at a loss this year. He'd overpaid for the company and now it was likely it would never pan out.

Was he really doing the same thing with Elements Computer Technologies?

Lucy sighed and dug around in her bag. "Here. I already printed it all out for you. Here's the numbers. The money never lies."

She handed him a thick file of papers. They weighed heavier in his hands than just paper. It was the entire company in his hands.

"Thank you, Lucy."

"I know you, Boss," she replied, standing from the table. She fixed her gaze on him. "I've worked hard on this. Please do the right thing here. Don't stop the move."

She picked up her things and returned her tray to its station. She didn't wait for Nathan to follow her before heading out of the cafeteria area and heading toward the next meeting. That was Lucy. Always ready for the next meeting.

Nathan set the file on the table with a thud. He thought about hiding in the R&D department again, but there were still more meetings he was expected to run. Everything felt overwhelming and he wished he could have a different life. He sighed with dread.

So he did the one thing he knew would make him feel better. He pulled out his phone and checked his bank accounts.

They were coming back up. It was no longer thirty million down. He was now at a mere ten million dollar loss. That was something he could handle. It made him feel a little bit better.

Money always did that. It didn't care if he was stressed or

sad. Money didn't care if he was angry or happy. It just was. Money was his constant. He knew where he stood with money. Money never let him down.

Nathan slid his phone back into his pocket and stood. He tucked the file under his arm. It was time to go back to work. It was only a few more hours until he got to see Holly again.

And somehow, that thought comforted him more than his bank account did.

CHAPTER 33

*H*olly

"Ms. Jones! Ms. Jones!" Preston ran yelling from the back of the room. Holly immediately made a mental note of where the first aid kit was and which route was the fastest to the office. Preston sounded legitimately concerned.

"What is it, Preston?" Holly asked, going down to one knee.

"Laurie is violating my religious rights," he told her. He wiped at his cheek.

"Your religious rights?" Holly asked, no longer worrying about the first aid kit.

"Yeah. She says Santa isn't real."

Oh boy. Holly thought to herself. She still had to stifle a laugh, though.

"How about we just don't talk to Laurie for the rest of the day?" Holly suggested. She made one mental note to email Preston's parents and another mental note on an already very long list to talk to Laurie about telling the other kids about Santa.

Winter break was all of ten minutes away and Holly could hardly stand the wait. The kids were antsy as well. They were ready to run outside. The big Holiday Parade was tomorrow, and everyone was excited. Then it was Christmas Eve and on to Christmas.

And best of all was dinner with Nathan in a few hours. She was actually more excited about that then she was for Christmas.

She looked at the clock. Eight minutes.

"Ms. Jones? If we move, will I ever see you again?" Kellie asked, her green eyes big and full of tears. She wiped at a freckled nose.

"I don't know," Holly answered. "I hope so, though."

Kellie's lower lip trembled. Holly had already had several kids burst into tears today at the thought of leaving everything they knew for a new city.

She needed to get them through these last few minutes.

The kids were standing at the ready. Everyone already had on coats and hats. Backpacks were full to bursting with all the year's art projects and homework assignments. The energy in the room was palpable. Holly needed to do something or the kids were going to rebel.

That's when she saw the snow. They were just tiny flakes, more rain than actual snow, but it was enough.

"Everyone outside!" she yelled, closing the buttons on her jacket. "Last five minutes is recess!"

The kids streamed out of her classroom and into the yard. Most of the parents were already there and waiting for their kids, so she was able to safely see her students off. Those who rode the buss sprinted to the waiting yellow caravans, ready to be free of the school's reach.

Holly waited for the last of her students to get safely away with parents or friends before heading back inside to finish cleaning up her classroom. She shivered as she closed the door behind her. The temperature was dropping as the flakes came down.

Most of the work was already done. She'd been prepping all week for the end of the year. Now, she just went around the room and removed the last few things that needed to come down. The snowflakes, some artwork, and their reading log for the year. She would put up new things once January and the new semester rolled around.

The room looked bare and strange without the decorations. She checked her watch. Still another hour and a half until dinner with Nathan. She could leave the school, but home would be cold. The school was warmer and had better internet.

She sat in her chair and spun around in lazy circles for a few moments before actually deciding to do it.

She picked up her phone, opened her web browser, and put in a job search for California.

It's just looking, she told herself. There's no harm in seeing what's available.

She wasn't sure she was actually okay with the idea of moving to California. Granted, many of her students would be there with the company moving, so that would be a plus. But, her dad would still be in Colorado, just without the anchor of the store.

She looked around her classroom and felt guilt paint her soul. She loved it here. She loved this school, her town, and this job.

She could go for a new apartment, but other than that, she was happy. She didn't want to move.

But she might. For him.

It was at least something to consider. Holly browsed the job opportunities and searched out a neighborhood that she could afford to live in. She checked out how close she would be to the beach, and that idea was at least tempting.

Could she give up the mountains for the beach? She wasn't sure.

She saved the job search and closed the browser on her phone. That was enough for today.

It was time for dinner.

NATHAN WAS WAITING for her at the restaurant. She'd picked her favorite Italian place, a cute little family owned place just off of Main Street. They had an intimate candle-lit table for two. Nathan already had glasses of wine out for them.

"You better be careful," she told him, settling into her chair. "A girl could get used to this."

Nathan grinned. His eyes glowed in the candlelight and drew Holly to them with their light. She was a moth to their flame.

"Maybe that's my evil plan," he replied.

"Step one: buy the girl dinner. Step two: do it again. Step three: take over the world." Holly nodded thoughtfully. "It seems like it could work."

Nathan chuckled and held up his wine glass for a cheers. She happily clinked her glass against his and took a sip. It was delicious. Definitely not just the house red.

"I wanted to ask you something," Nathan said, carefully setting his glass down on the white tablecloth. The candle-light flickered against the wine, creating beautiful patterns on the cloth.

"Anything," Holly replied.

"I'm thinking about keeping ECT here," he said, watching her face.

Holly's eyes went big and a smile filled her face. "Really?"

"Shh." He glanced around. "It's not official yet."

"But you're really going to do it?"

"The connection with the university is too good to lose. The staff is happy here and we can keep salaries priced for this area rather than trying to compete with the Bay Area," he explained. "The more I think about it, the more I know it's the right decision."

Holly grinned at him.

"When I asked you to look into it, I didn't think you were actually going to change the decision of the company," Holly said softly. "Thank you."

"Don't thank me yet," he warned. "I still have to run this by the board of directors. I may be the official owner, but they are the ones that set the rules."

"Thank you anyway," she told him. "It means a lot."

Nathan reached across the table and squeezed her hand. "It also means that I'll be here more."

Her grin widened. "Really?"

Maybe she didn't have to look for jobs in California after all.

"I'd have to spend most of my time at the Paradigm headquarters, but I would have a good reason to come out here more often," he replied. He made a nonchalant shrug. "Maybe we could hang out or something."

She laughed. "Yeah. We could go to football game."

Nathan laughed, squeezing her hand. "Basketball. Not football."

Holly took a sip of her wine, using it to give her courage. "You're not doing this for me, are you?" she asked him.

He smiled at her, his eyes dark and soft in the candlelight. "You're a perk. You are the cherry on top. The sundae is the company being successful here. George struck gold with his college recruitment. He said, 'get them before they know they're talent.' And he's absolutely right. It's brilliant. There's so much potential for growth, and I have these ideas for a new... Why are you smiling at me like that?"

Holly was grinning from ear to ear. "Because you sound so excited about it. Like you came up with a solution to a difficult puzzle. You haven't talked about your job once like this since I met you. But, right now, I can see that you love it."

"I love parts of it," he replied. "I like the idea of starting some new tech here. Elements has the setup I need to bring a new plan to the market."

"And there's that enthusiasm again," Holly said.

She liked seeing him like this. He was alive with idea. She could see how he ran a business as big as Paradigm when he was like this. He was all energy and dreams.

"To be honest, it's the first I've been excited for a while," he admitted. "I don't want to run the business. I'm not a great businessman, but Elements has the tech that can change things. I love working with that. I've been more excited to go to that office and play in the R&D department than anything else."

"Do you like your job?" Holly asked him, tilting her head to the side.

Nathan looked at her surprised. "Usually."

"Usually?" she asked. "You just said this is the first you've been excited in a while."

Nathan looked thoughtful. "Honestly? I hate the meetings. Being a CEO isn't what I love," he admitted. "I miss creating things. Creating solutions. I miss that."

"And you can't do that?" Holly asked.

"Not if I'm CEO," Nathan replied. "And it's the money that matters. So, I'll be CEO."

"Is that part of why you're keeping the company here?" she asked. "Because you can create things again?"

"Maybe. There's something magical there," he told her. "I'm probably boring you."

She shook her head. "The exact opposite. You're excited and I love seeing that. Tell me more. I want to know why you're excited."

He grinned. "Really?"

Holly nodded. She knew she wouldn't understand half the techno-jargon that was about to come out of his mouth, but she loved his enthusiasm. His eyes lit up and his hands moved around. Everything about him became more animated. It was like making love to him without having sex. Just excitement.

"Okay. But, you can't tell anyone about the plans," he said, keeping his voice low. "I still have to run them past the board."

Holly pretended to zip her mouth and turn a key. The motion made Nathan chuckle.

"Okay. So, I have this idea for the laptop case that will allow better airflow and cooling properties with a minimal adjustment needed...."

Holly nodded, catching only half of the words, but loving watching him explain his ideas to her. He was alive with ideas and she felt herself falling even more in love with this man.

Which was okay now because he would be staying here.

CHAPTER 34

*H*olly

"YOU'RE COMING to the parade today, right?" Holly whispered, her head cradled on Nathan's bare shoulder. He smoothed her hair with his hand against his head. The room was still blissfully dark with only the edges of the curtains showing any hint of morning light.

"I am. I made sure to schedule it with Lucy and everything," he replied.

She grinned, snuggling into him. This was heaven. She was warm, safe, and completely satisfied. If it weren't the fact that she'd been looking forward to this parade for the last month, she would happily stay in bed with Nathan for the rest of her life.

She wondered what their future looked like. Would there be more days like this? She knew it wouldn't be perfect or easy, nothing worth having ever was, but she hoped there would be days like this. Perfect, content days.

"What are you doing for Christmas? Since you're working, will you be staying here?" Holly asked.

Nathan shrugged beneath her. "I think so. Would you like me to stay?"

She sat up and rolled to her side, turning so that he could see her full face in the dim light. "Yes. Very much."

He grinned, his eyes still sleepy and soft. He looked younger, less troubled. There was a restfulness to him this morning that she found calming. He looked as happy as she felt.

"Then I'll stay," he said.

She kissed his cheek and then resettled into the hollow of his shoulder. "I can't wait to show you the party. My dad dresses up like Santa and gives out gifts. There's a potluck this year and Mrs. Stone promised to make her pumpkin pie. It's exactly what Christmas should be."

"As long as you're there, I'm happy," he told her.

She sighed with contentment, her cheek warm against his skin.

"You're going to be late," he warned her. "It's almost eight."

"I know," she said, wishing that time would just stop for a little bit longer. "I just don't want to leave. It feels so good here."

She could feel him smile at her in the dark as his arms gave her a squeeze.

"Get up. You've been looking forward to this."

She propped herself up on one shoulder and looked at him. "Thanks."

"You can show me just how grateful you are later," he said with a wink. She smacked his shoulder, but knew that she would happily "show him some appreciation" later. He had a body that made appreciating feel good.

She took one last comfortable breath, steeled herself for the cold of the room, and left the bed.

Except, Nathan had turned up the heat. The floor wasn't ice beneath her feet and she didn't immediately pop out in goose flesh upon leaving the blanket. She took her time heading to the bathroom and cleaning up. This time she had a fresh change of clothes and a real brush.

She came out looking like she'd spent the night at home, other than the glow he gave her. She couldn't wipe the goofy smile off her face.

He was up and dressed in dark slacks and a white dress shirt. He kissed her and handed her a cup of to-go coffee.

"Have a great day," he said, kissing her temple.

"I could really, really get used to this," she told him.

He just grinned at her.

She kissed him once more and hurried out the door to get to the parade.

THE PARADE STAGING ground was a mess. Someone had already given out one of the bags of candy that the floats were supposed to hand out. Now, kids in various holiday themed costumes were running around everywhere already hyped up on sugar.

Holly and Aliyah stood at the parade start line and evaluated the chaos. They were in charge of getting everyone ready to go. Once the parade started, Ms. Chellie was in charge so that Holly and Aliyah could ride on the floats.

"You ready for this?" Aliyah asked, tugging her hat down to cover her ears. It looked like she was a soldier preparing her helmet for war. Her eyes were fierce.

Holly took a deep breath and charged in.

"Zoe, I need you to get the floats lined up. Clancy, you

stop hitting your brother. You do it again and we will be having a discussion, understand? Lilibeth, your mom is just over by the coffee station. Fred, I need more candy on float three."

It came easily. She had been planning this for the last two months. She knew the parade route inside out and upside down. She knew each parade float and which kids were supposed to be where. Now, it was just a matter of getting everyone to where they were supposed to be.

Time flew by as she hurried between floats and checked in with the various crews. The fire department was running late since a Christmas tree went up in flames over on Elm street. The family was okay, and the house was saved, but Holly needed to move two floats up so that the fire truck could squeeze in when they got back.

She felt on top of the world. She felt like she could handle anything the world threw at her today. There was nothing that was going to knock her down. She had this. This was going to be a perfect Christmas day.

"I think we've got things rolling!" Aliyah told her, jogging past with a trio of lost kids. "You should head to your dad's float. We did it!"

Holly grinned and gave her a big thumbs up. She checked in with Ms. Chellie on her walkie-talkie and headed to her float. It was now time for the fun part of the parade.

"Hey kiddo," her dad called from his float as she passed.

"Hi, Dad!" She waved and came over to give him a hug. He was wearing his Santa costume and had his fluffy white beard in place.

"You look happy this morning," he said, returning her hug. He looked over her face and smiled. "I don't know the last time I've seen you look this happy."

"Really?"

He nodded. "It suits you. I like it."

That made her smile, and she realized that she was already grinning. So, she just smiled a little wider.

"Thanks, Dad." She looked around. "How's the float?"

He shrugged. "It'll probably be the last year for this old gal," he said sadly. "The tree needs replacing and some squirrels got into the presents last night. I managed to fix them, but they won't make it another year. Seems to be the story of my world."

Holly's smile faltered slightly.

"Don't stop smiling because of me," her dad said, seeing her face. "I'm okay. These things happen. It's okay. You keep that smile."

Holly's heart ached. She could see the tiredness in her father's eyes. The lifetime of work that he was seeing slowly fall apart and that he couldn't put back together again.

She glanced around. Most of the parade participants were on their floats, so it was quiet. The two bookstore employees were getting coffee, so they were alone. Holly hoisted herself up onto the float.

"Dad, I have some good news for you," she whispered. "You can't tell anyone because it isn't official yet, but it might make your day better."

Her dad frowned, the white Santa beard shifting on his face. "What do you mean?"

She looked around one more time. "Nathan is planning on keeping Elements here. He wants to stop the move to California," she whispered.

Light entered her father's eyes. "Really?" His voice cracked with hope.

"Really. But you can't tell anyone. Promise me you won't tell."

"Not a soul," he promised, but his smile was already speaking volumes. Tears of joy welled up in his eyes. "I can't tell you how happy that makes me."

"I know. It means you can keep the store open," Holly said, her own voice growing thick with emotion.

He hugged her close. "Thank you for telling me, Holly. It's made my Christmas."

Her heart filled with joy. That was what Christmas was really about. Making people joyful.

"Oh, look, here comes our hero now," Mark said, pointing down the road.

Nathan walked among the floats, his black coat open in the cool air. She grinned and hopped off the float to greet him.

"I thought you weren't coming until the parade started," she said, greeting him with a hug and a smile.

"Well, I had no one to have meetings with. It seems everyone who works at Elements is here. It's hard to have a meeting without employees," Nathan replied with a smile.

Her walkie-talkie chirped and several engines started around them. The parade was starting.

She grinned at him. "You want to ride on the float with me?"

His eyes went wide. "I can do that?"

"Yes, Mr. Big-shot. You can do that." She jumped up onto the float bed with her father. The float was made to look like Santa's study with a Christmas tree, presents, and a rocking chair for Santa to sit. There were spaces for two more adults to sit and throw candy from the sides.

"What do I do? I've never been in a parade before," Nathan said, carefully taking his spot.

"It's easy," Mark told him. "You just throw candy at the kids. Just not too hard."

Nathan grinned like a little kid. The trucks around them rumbled forward and the parade began. The sounds of the marching band drums reverberated off the buildings and the brass of their horns echoed down the streets.

The float moved forward, turning off the alley and onto the official parade route.

Holly threw candy and waved to the kids. She recognized many of them from school and made sure to wave and call to them. But her real attention was on Nathan. He was having the time of his life.

He threw out massive handfuls of candy, not realizing that he was burning through the bag at an alarming rate. He was having so much fun she didn't want to tell him to stop. The smile on his face was like that of a kid on Christmas morning.

He looked over at Holly and gave her such a smile that her heart nearly stopped in her chest. It was the happiest she'd ever seen a person look. He winked at her and then went back to throwing candy out for the children.

The town waved and cheered for him, as if they knew he was going to save them. How could he not after being here for a week? People called out to him and waved with smiles.

She looked over at her father. He sat in his Santa chair waving and ho-ho-hoing with glee. The sparkle was back in his eyes. His shoulders were taller. He had his hope back again.

All around them, Christmas music echoed down the streets, intermingling with the sounds of children's delight.

This was Christmas to Holly. This was joy and wonder. The spirit of hope and community.

And then it started to snow, just like magic.

CHAPTER 35

*N*athan

NATHAN COULDN'T REMEMBER the last time he was this happy.

He couldn't remember the last time that his mind had felt this unfettered and his soul didn't feel like it needed to escape his body.

And it was all because of Holly.

She was magic. She was everything he wanted. And right now, he had a glimpse of a beautiful future.

He would continue to work on Elements. She would come and visit him in California, and he would show her everything the state had to offer. For once, he was excited to share his wealth with someone and not be worried that they would try and take advantage of him. He knew Holly would never do that.

Then he would purchase a house here in Devonsville. They would move in together after an acceptable amount of time, but sooner rather than later because her apartment was tiny. They would build a life together. They would live happily ever after.

He could see it all coming together like something out of a fairy tale. He was Prince Charming and she was his snow bunny princess.

And so, he threw candy to children and hummed along to Christmas carols. He thought about attending the candlelight service for Christmas Eve at the local church. It seemed like he should thank some higher power for this happiness in his life.

He could see community everywhere he looked. People were being helpful and kind to one another. The Christmas spirit of kindness and generosity was everywhere he looked. As he gazed out from the parade float, he could see it.

And he actually could feel it. He was a part of it for the first time in a very long time.

The parade ended and the float returned to its spot behind the bookstore. Nathan helped Mark down from the platform. Mark thanked him and started bringing in the decorations from the float. Holly sat on the edge, her feet hanging off and swinging.

"That was great," he told her. "Thank you for letting me be on the float."

She grinned at him. "You looked like you were having a blast. I was afraid we were going to run out of candy there for a while."

He chuckled. "I did too," he admitted. "I was a little overzealous at first."

"You figured it out," she told him, pride in her smile.

He went over and put his hands on her waist, intending on helping her down, but instead she leaned forward and kissed him. Her hair spilled around him and she tasted like candy. Snow sparkled in the air around them.

She grinned at him and he helped her down, his knees

shaky with emotion. How did she do this to him? She made him feel things. She made him happy.

"I just need to check on a few things with the parade, and then we can go grab some lunch," she told him.

"Okay. Ill be in the bookstore."

He went in through the back door and wandered the shelves. It smelled of ink and paper, mixed with a hint of coffee and fresh baked goods. The quiet chatter of the coffee shop filled the air as he made his way to the front and ordered a cup of coffee. He sat by the window and watched the last of the parade goers meander around the streets.

Holly wore a bright red knit hat that made her easy to spot. She was talking to a police officer and smiling as she helped him take down the road blocks for the parade. He loved watching her.

His phone pinged and he looked down. It was an update on the stock market.

Normally, he would open it and read it, checking his accounts and seeing how his money was doing. His money was the first thing on his mind and these alerts were important to keeping track of just how much he had made for the day.

His hand twitched, his fingers moving to open the app that would tell him what he was worth. But he paused. He looked out the window at Holly and she waved to him.

He didn't open the app. He put his phone back in his pocket and relaxed back into his chair. He let himself sip his coffee and not worry what he was worth right at this very moment. He could check it later. There was a meeting with Lucy and some accountant for the company later today, and he'd find out his worth then.

Holly ran across the street and came into the coffee shop. Her cheeks and nose were red with the cold, matching her knit hat.

"I'm going to be late for lunch," she told him. "One of the floats is stuck and they need me to help. I'm really sorry, but..."

"Don't worry about it," he smiled. He stood up and kissed her cheek. Her skin was cool against his lips. "We're still on for dinner, right?"

She nodded, her smile coming back. "Definitely."

"Then I will see you then."

"Thank you. See you in a bit!" She flashed him one last smile before running back out into the cold winter weather. He watched her for a moment before gathering his things.

If he hurried, he could still get into the R&D department before anyone noticed. He had a little time before his next meeting, and if he skipped lunch, he could easy get some good work time in. His fingers itched to play with the laptop and see if the design in his head would work the way he thought it would.

He sent a message to Hal to get the car ready. Nathan buttoned up his jacket and stepped out of the shop. The cold stung at his face and hands, but he smiled at everyone he passed.

Today was going to be a great day. He was genuinely happy. He felt like singing Christmas carols as he headed to the car, except Hal was driving and he didn't want to annoy the poor man.

The car was warm and ready for him. Hal was in the driver seat as Nathan took his usual spot in the back. Gregory had shotgun today. He'd been the one chasing Nathan all over the city.

"Next time, warn me if you're going to join a parade," Gregory told him, grabbing a tissue and dabbing at his nose. "You're going to give me a heart attack trying to keep you safe in a public place like that."

Guilt tugged on Nathan. "I'm sorry. I didn't think."

Gregory waved his hand. "To be honest, it looked like fun. And you looked like a kid."

"I have wanted to be in a parade like that for as long as I can remember," Nathan admitted. "I can't believe I've never done it before."

Gregory grunted as Hal started driving.

"What's that supposed to mean?" Nathan asked him.

"It's her," Gregory told him. "She's the one making your dreams come true."

Nathan paused to consider it, and found that to be true. Holly was making his dreams come true.

"Please don't start singing. Or whistling. Or humming," Hal begged, glancing back at him in the rear view mirror. "You can't pick a key and stay in it."

Nathan was tempted to burst out in some sort of love song just to annoy him, but as the man was in control of the car, he decided against it.

Nathan passed the short drive thinking about the upgrades he wanted to make. He was torn between working on a new processor or if adding RAM would simply be enough for what he wanted. Either way, he couldn't wait to get into the department and get his hands on some tech and play.

The car pulled up to the front of the building and Gregory and Nathan got out. Gregory became Nathan's silent shadow once more as they entered the glass building. The lobby was empty as everyone was at the parade.

Empty, except for Lucy.

She stood, hand on hips, dressed in dark red and with murder in her eyes.

"There you are," she scolded. "Where have you been?"

Nathan frowned, not understanding. There was no meetings until later in the day. He'd double checked.

"What do you mean?" he asked her.

"I messaged you. We need to talk," she said. "Didn't you get my text?"

Nathan fumbled for his phone and found two missed messages from Lucy. He had been so caught up in designing the laptop in his head, he'd neglected his phone entirely.

"Wow. She's even more in your head than I thought," Lucy said, crossing her arms. He knew she was referencing Holly. The way she said it twisted Nathan the wrong way. No one should talk about Holly like that.

"What do you want, Lucy?" Nathan asked her. He could feel his time in the R&D department slipping away from him.

"We need to talk. In private." She turned on her heel and began walking. "Follow me."

Nathan raised an eyebrow and glanced at Gregory.

Gregory grunted.

Nathan had to agree Gregory was right. Don't mess with an angry woman. Just do as she says.

So he followed her.

Her heels clicked on the tile floor as they crossed the main lobby and went past a row of empty desks. A little Christmas tree stood flickering off to the side, but Lucy passed it without a second glance. She headed straight for George Element's office.

Once inside, she settled in George's big leather chair.

"Have a seat," she told him. Except she was sitting in the power seat. That left Nathan having to sit in the lesser chairs on the opposite side of the desk.

Instead he remained standing. He crossed the large room and looked at George's bookcase. There were many photographs of the man, but none of his family. It was always just him in exotic locals, with over-sized fish, meeting celebrities, or posing in famous locations.

For some reason, it made Nathan sad. He knew the man had children. He had a family. Yet, in this office there was no indication of it. There was no love in this office for anything other than the job.

"What did you want to talk about?" Nathan asked her, taking a relaxed lean against a wall.

Lucy crossed her legs and glared at him.

"This company is moving to California." She said it with authority.

"Is that so?" Nathan raised his eyebrows. "Since when did you become CEO?"

"Don't play with me, Nathan," Lucy warned. "I've spent months making this happen. I did everything for this acquisition."

Nathan didn't say anything. It was true. He'd given most of the responsibility to Lucy. He'd been busy trying to salvage RentTech and failing. He had only just started looking at Elements, even though it was technically his job.

"I understand that you've put a lot of effort into this," he replied. "And I'll make sure that you're compensated. But the company should stay here."

Lucy laughed, but it had no joy. "And why is that? To make your little princess happy? So that you can come in and be her white knight? So you can save the town?"

Nathan didn't say anything.

"Nathan, I have put too much work into this. I've made deals and promises. I'm not letting you take this from me," Lucy said. Her dark eyes glittered with anger as she looked at him. "The company is moving."

Righteous indignation filled Nathan's chest. He didn't like being told what to do.

"No." Nathan shook his head. "It's not. I choose what happens with this company, not you. You don't dictate what I do with my company."

Lucy sighed. "I didn't want to have to do this, Nathan. I

don't want to have this fight with you, but you aren't seeing reason."

She stood up and crossed the room. Despite the fact that she was a good head shorter than him, she managed to look down at him.

He was ready to destroy her. She was as good as fired for this. This was unacceptable to him. How dare Lucy usurp him like this? Fury began to vibrate in his chest, steam heating in his ears.

"I will go to the board with this." Lucy spoke softly, but without hesitation. "I will tell them how this mess happened. You are already on shaky ground with them for RentTech. They will destroy you for this. You will lose everything."

It was like being hit with a bucket of cold water. The fire in his belly vanished immediately. She wasn't bluffing and she was going for the jugular.

He knew the board would fire him if she went to them. They would take his job. The board had been looking for excuses to get rid of him after the RentTech debacle, and this would be a perfect excuse to fire him.

"You wouldn't," he whispered.

Lucy stared up defiantly. "I would. For this, I would."

The betrayal hurt. Nathan had thought they were a team.

"I'm sorry, Nathan. I like you, but I like money more," Lucy told him, reading his thoughts. "You taught me that. Money is everything."

Her words hung in the air, haunting him.

Money was everything.

Or was it?

"This is a wake-up call, Nathan. You need to get back to what you are good at," Lucy told him. "You need to head back to California and do your damn job. Things will go as planned. We'll make money. That's what matters."

Nathan nodded. His head spun. Usually, he was the one in

control. He was the CEO, the boss. How had he let this happen? How had he lost his way in this?

"Nathan, we'll make money." Lucy touched his shoulder, her voice soft and kinder now. "That's what's important, right?"

"Right." Money was what was important. It was what drove him. It was what had always driven him.

"Okay." Lucy smiled. "Your flight is scheduled in four hours. I already had Gregory pack your things. That should still give you enough time for dinner with what's-her-name."

"Holly. Her name's Holly."

What was he going to tell Holly? He could still see her smile when he told her the company was staying. She would be crushed. Her students, her father's bookstore, her town... he was taking it all away from her.

"Sure." Lucy shrugged. She frowned at his expression. "It's going to be okay, Nathan. We're going to make millions. Money is everything, remember?"

"Right." He hoped he sounded more sure than he felt.

Lucy sighed, her face concerned.

"Boss, can I make a suggestion?" She put her hand on his shoulder.

"What? You have more companies you want to move?"

"The girl. She's not good for you," Lucy told him. "She's got you all sentimental. You aren't making sound business decisions because of her. It's not like you. You don't give up money for anyone."

"What do you mean?"

"I mean, you aren't yourself. Two weeks ago, you were a bloodthirsty shark. Today, you're all cuddly and soft. You want to keep a business here because it's the nice thing to do," Lucy explained. "You can't run a business and be *nice*."

Nathan sighed. He had felt the same thing. He wasn't

hungry for the thrill of seeing his bank account numbers go up like he used to be.

"I think you need to choose between her and your business." Lucy squeezed his arm. "I don't mean to be cruel, but I want to be honest. I'm here to help you make money, remember? And she's not helping you with that."

"I know," Nathan admitted. "I'm not thinking about the business when I'm with her."

"And that's a problem if you want to make money," Lucy said. "It's already a problem, but it's just going to get worse."

She grabbed a pen, scribbled something and handed him a slip of paper. It was big number and lots of zeros.

"That's the projection," Lucy told him. "That's all going to be yours if you choose the company."

Millions. Millions of dollars. He'd have an even bigger bank account. He felt the usual thrill of seeing money in his account. This would fix all the loses. This would make him happy. He knew it. Money always made him happy.

"Money is everything," he repeated.

"Money is everything," Lucy agreed.

CHAPTER 36

*N*athan

NATHAN SAT in the empty office, staring at his bank account numbers on his phone.

He was down ten million today, but the market looked like it might swing up by the end of the day. A ten million dollar fluctuation was nothing, but it was worrying. He hadn't had a good up day since meeting Holly.

He could see the choice in front of him. Holly or the money.

The money had always been there for him. Since the beginning, money had given him what he needed. It wasn't his family that had made him successful, it was the fact that he liked seeing the numbers in his bank account go up.

He wished he could have both worlds, one of business and one with community and friends. He knew it couldn't be. It had to be one or the other. That was the way it had always been, and up until this moment, the easy choice had been the money.

He wanted to forget the smiles on the children's faces today. He wanted to forget the warmth of the town. The way everyone said hello and treated him like he'd always lived there. He wanted to pretend that taking this business away wouldn't change the town. That it would stay the same.

But he knew it wouldn't.

ECT was the lifeblood of the town. Without it, the majority of the high-paying jobs would disappear. The housing market was already experiencing a downturn because so many houses were being put on the market for the move to California.

"Money is what matters," he told himself.

The money would be worth it. He would see his bank account and this would be justified.

Except, he knew that the money didn't matter for Holly.

He mattered to her.

He closed his eyes and tried to imagine what the next few months would look like.

The company would move to California. He would be busy with molding it into what Paradigm wanted. He would gut ECT and change everything about it to fit the Paradigm model. It wouldn't be the company Holly remembered when he was done.

In California, he would barely see Holly at all. He would go back to his old life. The one where he slept at the office and only ate because Lucy brought him food. He would barely have time to shower, let alone have a relationship.

It wasn't fair to Holly. She deserved someone who would love and cherish her. She deserved someone who could volunteer in her classroom. Who could be in parades and sit and discuss books, who could lay in bed and snuggle and laugh.

He wasn't that person.

This week had been heavenly, but it wasn't who he was. He was Paradigm Technologies. He was a cut-throat businessman who took what he want. His only concern was money, and getting more of it.

He could give Holly money, but that wasn't what she needed.

She needed love and time.

He didn't know how to do that. Not with his life. Not with the way his world worked.

He'd let himself believe the dream. He'd let himself think that if he kept ECT in Devonsville, it would change things. That he could have both worlds.

But he couldn't.

He could only have one.

He had to end things. If he did it now, they would both survive the heartbreak. She would have her family and Christmas to help her through it. He didn't want to ruin her Christmas with memories of him.

He was the Grinch. Scrooge. The enemy of Christmas. It was better for her to have the holiday without him ruining things. Better to leave before the stakes were too high. If he left now, she could still have a happy Christmas.

Better to wake from the dream than have it turn into a nightmare.

His hands went to his head, his heart aching with the choice. A tear trickled down his cheek.

He held his phone in his hands, cradling the numbers he could see there. The decision was made and he was choosing wealth.

It would be worth it, he told himself.

The money always was.

Money was what mattered.

CHAPTER 37

$\mathcal{M}$erryweather

SOMETHING WAS WRONG. Merryweather could feel the shift in her bones, much like the ache in her joints before a big storm. She could feel the magic starting to fade.

Darkness was coming.

The love was fading.

Something had to be done.

CHAPTER 38

$\mathcal{H}$olly

"THERE," Holly whispered, carefully placing the last piece of tape.

She smiled at her work. The wrapping paper was neatly folded around the corners and she'd even made the tape look nice. She wrote Nathan's name in neat print on the corner. It was possibly the best wrapping she'd ever done on a present.

It was just a copy of *A Christmas Carol*, but it seemed like the perfect Christmas Eve present for Nathan. She'd agonized over which book to get him for the Christmas Eve tradition, but had finally settled on this one.

It was tradition in her family to gift a book on Christmas eve. She was excited to share this tradition with Nathan. She was excited to share everything with him.

Life was good. She tucked the book under the small tree in her apartment next to the other gift she'd picked out for him. It was just a t-shirt with the name of the town and a printed mountain background. It wasn't much, but she thought he would like it since he was moving his company here. It felt like a good gift and she couldn't wait for Christmas to come so she could give it to him.

Half the fun of Christmas was giving gifts. She knew he wouldn't be expecting anything, which made it even better. She felt a little like Santa Claus.

It was time for dinner with Nathan. She smoothed her black dress down and checked her earrings. She'd even curled her hair and put on makeup since it was supposed to be a nice dinner. They had reservations at Mountainside, which was one of the nicer restaurants in town. The last time she'd eaten there was for a wedding.

COLD WIND BLEW as Holly hurried into the restaurant. The hostess told her that Nathan hadn't arrived yet, but was happy to take her to the table. They had a small, romantic table in a corner. A small candle flickered on the table, and two pristine white napkins sat ready and folded.

A thought hit Holly.

"Can I order two glasses of champagne?" she asked the server.

The champagne arrived and Holly sat waiting patiently for Nathan to arrive. With her hands in her lap, she watched the tiny bubbles in the golden liquid dance to the top. She checked her watch and found that he was ten minutes late. She chewed her lip before remembering that she had lipstick on.

Had he forgotten? She checked her phone, but didn't see any messages saying he'd gotten tied up in a meeting. She hoped that he was okay. The roads could be icy this time of year. Every time the front door opened, she perked up, hoping it was him.

Nathan arrived nearly twenty minutes late. He walked through the restaurant with a cool confidence.

Holly stood up to greet him. "Hi," she said, coming to kiss him. He sat before she could.

There was a darkness to his eyes that she hadn't seen before. It didn't match the smiling joy she'd seen earlier that day.

It must have been a rough day, she decided.

"I ordered us a couple of glasses of champagne," she said, motioning to the delicate glasses on the table. "I don't know when you plan to make the announcement about Elements, but I thought we could celebrate a little tonight. Just the two of us."

She smiled at him, hoping that now that he was sitting in the warm restaurant, he might relax and have a better evening. He didn't smile back.

"Is everything okay?" she asked him. "If you don't want champagne, they have some amazing cocktails here."

Nathan's jaw twitched. "ECT isn't staying in Devonsville," he said, his voice flat.

Holly's smile faltered. "What do you mean? You sounded so sure earlier."

"I mean the company is moving to California," he replied.

"Oh." Holly's shoulders fell. She immediately thought of her father. He'd been so excited to hear he might be able to keep his bookstore running. She thought of her students. Nearly a quarter of her class was preparing for the move to California. They were scared and unsure of changing homes. Moving was hard on kids. "Is there a reason why?"

"Because I said so," he said sharply. "I own this business. I can do whatever I want with it."

Holly pulled back at the sharp tone. He'd never spoken to

her like that. He sounded angry with her, but Holly couldn't figure out why. She hadn't done anything wrong, at least not that she could think of.

"Okay." She fiddled with the napkin in her lap. "How was the rest of your day?"

"I don't want to talk about it," he snapped at her. He reached out and drank his champagne without offering a toast. He didn't even look at her.

Holly was a patient person. She had to be as a second grade teacher. She was good at managing her emotions and not responding when people reacted poorly. Still, this grated on her nerves. Her nice night out with a charming date was turning sour.

He finished his champagne and made a face. "What kind of cheap champagne did you order?"

"I just ordered regular champagne," she said, surprised at the defensiveness in her own voice.

"It's terrible," he scolded her.

"Okay..." She picked up her menu and pretended to read it. Her eyes blurred with hurt tears that made her feel stupid. His sharp words shouldn't affect her like this, but still it stung to be spoken to like that. She blinked, trying to clear them so she could see if she wanted the filet mignon or the salmon.

To be honest, at this point she wasn't sure she wanted to eat at all.

She cleared her throat. "So, I thought we could go ice skating tonight," she said, setting her menu to the side and trying again. "It's this fun tradition in town to go ice skating the evening after the parade. It's just for couples and the rink hangs mistletoe in every corner. I thought it would be fun."

She had been looking forward to having a date for once to go with. It was usually full of teenagers and old married couples, but she could see her and Nathan having a wonderful time. Maybe it would even put him in a better mood.

"I'm leaving tonight," Nathan announced, not looking up from his menu.

"You're leaving?" Holly frowned, surprised. They'd made plans for Christmas Eve. She was looking forward to sharing her holiday traditions with him.

"Do I have to repeat everything?" He set down his menu and glared at her.

"No, but you can explain. We had plans." Holly tried to keep the irritation out of her voice.

"Business."

Anger flared up in Holly's chest. "That's it? Business?"

"I don't need to explain myself to you," he told her.

Holly's jaw dropped. Who was this man? This wasn't the Nathan she knew and loved. "No, you don't have to explain. But it would be polite."

Nathan focused his gaze on her, but instead of feeling like the center of the galaxy, she felt like a negligent vendor for his business.

"I have a business to run. I've spent too much time playing here. I have work to do."

"And Christmas? Our plans?" she asked, crossing her arms.

His jaw twitched again. "Business comes first."

Holly stared at him for a moment. Her eyes narrowed. "What's going on?" she asked. "This isn't like you."

His eyes flashed once. "It is like me. You just don't know me."

Holly's heart fell. "I guess not."

"I can't do this, Holly," he said, his voice going soft. "I have to go."

"Go?"

He stood up and reached for his wallet. "I'm sorry, Holly."

He placed a bill large enough to cover the champagne on the table. He then turned and left, putting on his coat as he walked through the restaurant. He left her.

Holly sat in shock for a moment. This wasn't how she'd seen this evening going at all. She stared at the champagne glasses, one empty and one full. What just happened?

She grabbed her coat and chased after him. The streetlights were just starting to flicker on as the winter sun dipped red behind dark clouds. The wind nipped at her, making her shiver and wish for a heavier jacket.

"Nathan, wait!" she called to him, chasing him down the street.

He turned, his brown eyes sad. She slowed, breathless beside him.

"Nathan, what's going on?"

He sighed. "Holly, go home. Enjoy the holiday with your family. Celebrate with your friends and the town."

"What about you?"

"I don't have Christmas," he told her. "I have my business. That's what I've always had. It's what I want."

"And us?"

He leaned over and kissed her cheek. "It was good while it lasted, but I'm not the one for you. I'll only end up hurting you."

"Nathan..." Holly shook her head. "No. Please."

"I'm letting you go," he told her. "It's my Christmas gift to you. I can't give up who I am, and I don't fit here. I don't fit in your life and you don't fit in mine. My company comes first, and you are so much better than second place."

"We could make it work," she said, but she knew it wasn't true. She'd seen what being a CEO did to George Element's wives. That wasn't something she was willing to sign up for. She didn't want to be second to the company.

There were a lot of things that she was willing to

compromise on. This wasn't one of them. It appeared that their initial reservations were correct.

They should have just left things at the ski resort. They both knew this was never actually going to work. It had been a silly dream to think otherwise. They were just too different and they both knew it.

Nathan was right. This needed to end here.

"Goodbye, Holly." Nathan kissed her cheek one last time. His lips were soft as they grazed her skin. "Thank you for this week."

She closed her eyes, not wanting to cry.

When she opened them, he was gone.

CHAPTER 39

*M*erryweather

MERRYWEATHER WATCHED as Nathan got on a plane and headed for California. Holly was no where in sight.

"Oh, fiddlesticks." Merryweather frowned. This was going to take some fixing.

She picked up the phone.

"Fauna? I need a favor," she said.

Her sister sighed. "You always need favors."

"Yes, but this one is worth it," Merryweather promised.

Fauna sighed, but at least she agreed to listen.

CHAPTER 40

*N*athan

"Mr. Reed?" a soft feminine voice asked at Nathan's office door. "I have some files for you. May I come in?"

"Sure," Nathan said, motioning forward. He was glad for the distraction. No matter what he did, he couldn't seem to be able to focus on work. His heart just wasn't in it.

The woman came in with a stack of files in her petite hands. She wore a black pant suit with a soft, pale green undershirt that brought out the light green color of her eyes. He wasn't sure what her age was. Her hair was so blonde it appeared to be almost silver against the black of her jacket.

"Why are you delivering files?" he asked as she set down the folder on his desk. "The mail-room usually handles that."

"I'm an intern," she explained. "And since it's Christmas Eve, there just isn't a lot to do right now. My boss said to find something to do."

"What's your name?" he asked her. Now that she was

here, he found he liked having some company and didn't want her to leave just yet. The office was too quiet today.

"Fauna," she replied. He thought he kept his face still, but she still chuckled at his expression. "I know it's kind of a unique name."

Now that he was looking at her, she looked vaguely familiar. There was something about her eyes, or maybe the color of her hair... "Have we met before?" he asked. "You look really familiar."

She shook her head. "Nope. But maybe you've run across my sisters."

"Maybe," he agreed. Long shadows filled the room as the daylight faded. "Why don't you head home? You can tell your boss I said you can go. It is Christmas Eve after all."

"Thanks, but it's okay. My flight home is late enough that I'm practically riding Santa's sleigh tonight. I might as well be here," Fauna said with a laugh. "Otherwise I'd just be at home watching old Christmas movies and eating popcorn. I don't need the calories."

"Thank you for the files," he said.

"No problem," Fauna replied. "Can I get you some coffee or anything? I can get hot or iced. I'm better at hot, though."

"No, thank you." Hot coffee made him think of colder climates. He thought of the coffee shop in the bookstore and wondered if Holly was there now.

She'd be getting things ready for the party. She'd been so excited about it. He hoped she was doing okay.

"Why the long face?" Fauna asked him.

He looked up in surprise. "What do you mean?"

She shrugged. "You just look sad. Maybe I can help." She pulled up one of his guest chairs and sat down. "I'm a really good problem solver. It's why I was hired."

"Thanks, but I think it's above your pay grade," he told her.

"Is it about Elements Computer Technologies?" she asked.

"What makes you say that?" he asked, her narrowing his eyes.

"The higher-ups were talking about it in the hall. They didn't know I was there," she explained.

"What did you hear?" he asked. It would be nice to know what the other employees were saying. No one seemed to give him real answers since he was the big boss. They always told him what they thought he wanted to hear.

"Just that the staff of ECT isn't excited about the move. There's a lot of talk about a lot of the main staff quitting," she replied. "And, some of the other department heads are wondering why Paradigm is adding another division here."

Nathan nodded listening. He'd heard similar rumors, but his course was set. He couldn't change things now even if he wanted to.

"And what do you think?" Nathan asked her, leaning back in his chair. He found that he liked her. It was nice to have someone to talk to today. The rest of the office was empty and he was tired of being alone. Talking with Fauna would be better than sitting and thinking of Holly and the things he couldn't have.

"You want my opinion?" Fauna looked thoughtful. "If I were in charge, I'd sell Elements to someone else. Paradigm already has three other divisions that do that work. It's overkill for the company and will just lead to resentment and redundancy. If you sold it to a smaller buyer, you wouldn't have to worry about it as competition. You could probably even sell it at a profit right now."

"I have to say I haven't heard that advice yet," Nathan told her.

She grinned. "I think outside of the box."

"Who do you think Paradigm should sell to?" Nathan asked. "Since you seem to have thought this out."

"You're going to laugh at my idea," she told him. "But, I'm going to tell you anyway."

"Go for it. I'll do my best not to laugh," he promised.

She looked at him with pale green eyes full of old knowledge. "You. You should buy it."

He couldn't help it. He did laugh. "Me? But I'm the CEO of Paradigm."

"You're also the creator of the Quad-Ram. Elements is known for new and unique solutions. Can you imagine if you were the owner? You wouldn't have to be the CEO and run things." She grinned at him.. "You could work in the company as and create things like the Quad-Ram again. It would be a perfect match."

Nathan shook his head. "And in your fantasy world, what happens to Paradigm?"

"They get a new CEO. There's plenty of people gunning for your job," she told him. "Some of the rumors, especially about RentTech, don't sound so good for you."

"Thanks for the warning," he said dryly. It wasn't anything he hadn't heard before. Everyone wanted to be the CEO. It was part of why he had to be ruthless.

She held up her hands. "Don't shoot the messenger," she said. "I'm just telling you what I've heard. Interns hear a lot of gossip since everyone seems to forget we're there until it's time for coffee."

Nathan had to agree. It was easy to forget that the interns were there, quietly working in the background.

"You hear anything else interesting?" he asked her.

"The board is meeting in an hour," she told him. "They say it's just for an end of the year thing."

Anxiety balled up in Nathan's stomach. He knew he had no reason to be nervous, yet there it was anyway. He pushed it away. He was making Paradigm money again. He had no reason to be nervous.

"Well, I should be getting back to work," Fauna said, rising gracefully to her feet. "Anyway, thanks for listening to my crazy idea. I'm actually a really big fan of the Quad-Ram. I'd love to see something like that again."

"Thanks for the files, and the crazy idea," Nathan told her, picking up the folder.

"Any time," Fauna replied. "Merry Christmas, Mr. Reed. I hope you get what you want."

"Thank you. You too."

She gave him one last smile before exiting his office.

He played with the folder in his hands, thinking over the conversation. His thoughts drifted to the laptop back at the Elements' R&D department. He still had ideas he wanted to try. Things that would change laptops forever.

What if...

He closed his eyes and let himself imagine what it might look like if he followed Fauna's idea. He could afford to purchase Elements easily. He even knew a couple of people who'd would make an excellent CEO. He imagined being able to go to the R&D department and simply work on new technologies without the stress and worry of running a company.

Granted, his bank account would suffer, but he was a billionaire. He had more money than he could really spend at this point, even with the purchase of Elements.

But, the part that stuck out to him most was that he could come home to Holly every night. He could have dinner with her whenever he wanted. They could talk about books and lay in bed all morning on Saturdays. He could help out at school functions and see the kids.

He thought about Molly, Jake, and Natasha. He wondered if Santa would be coming to their houses tonight. He thought about the parade and the town.

And he found that he ached for all of it.

He wanted it.

"But that's not what I chose," Nathan said aloud to no one in particular. Irritated, he pulled out his phone and opened the app for his bank accounts. He needed to be reminded what he was working for.

His fingers paused on the log-in screen. He found that he didn't actually care. That it didn't matter compared to Holly's smile. Instead of the bank account app, he opened his camera and scrolled through his pictures.

Holly's smile gave him the rush he was looking for. Her soft green eyes and laughing mouth gave him more happiness than seeing one-hundred million extra dollars in his bank account.

The money didn't matter.

Money wasn't everything.

Holly was.

Nathan's eyes snapped open. He knew what he needed to do.

He checked his watch. If what Fauna said was correct, he had ten minutes to get up to the board room and make his case. It was crazy, but he found himself excited for it.

For the first time all day, he had the energy and drive to do what needed to be done.

Now that the idea was in his mind, he wasn't going to be able to stop. He certainly couldn't stop the smile on his face or the laugh that started deep in his stomach and worked its way out into the world.

He was going to be happy.

He was going to make this a Christmas to remember.

CHAPTER 41

*H*olly

HOLLY SAT BEFORE A ROARING FIRE, watching the flames jump and dance around a yule log. She wondered if it would be appropriate to put another shot of rum in her hot cocoa or if three was already too many.

She wanted to feel happy. It was Christmas Eve. She was warm and full of good food. Her father had made his famous pot roast and she'd eaten enough mashed potatoes that she was probably at least fifty percent potato herself. There would soon be presents and cookies.

There was every reason to be happy and content. But, all she could think about was Nathan.

So, she sat on the floor in front of the fire and drank rum.

It was her annual place to sit on Christmas Eve. Holly and Mark had already watched the old Claymation version of Rudolf the Red-Nosed Reindeer. Now they would exchange books as was their tradition.

When Holly was a little girl, they used to do this every year. Her mother would pick out an educational book with beautiful pictures for her. One year, she got an encyclopedia of dragons. Another, it was a compendium of North American flowers. Once, she'd gotten the most amazing picture book full of deep sea fish. That was the last one her mother had given her.

Mark always picked a fiction book for Holly. One year it was *Lord of the Rings*. The years where new GRR Martin books came out, she knew exactly what book he would give her.

As a girl, she would crawl into bed after setting out cookies and milk and stare at the pictures before reading the book from her father. She'd read until her eyes gave out, and then she'd dream of dragons and flowers until it was time for Christmas presents.

This year, she sat ready with a book for her father. It was wrapped neatly in wrapping that matched the one still tucked under her tree at home. The fact that she'd left it there made her sad all over again.

"You doing okay?" Mark asked, joining her on the floor. He groaned slightly as he settled his old bones in front of the fire. "You need some more rum?"

She shook her head yes, feeling her brain slosh a little. She was tipsy, but she still needed to drive home. She could sleep here in her childhood bed, but she didn't want to cry into her childhood pillow. She was a grownup now.

"Here," her father said, handing her a brown paper package. "I think you'll like this one."

She set her mug to the side and carefully pulled open the paper. A beautiful leather bound book came out. *The Silmarillion* was emblazoned in gold leaf in beautiful flowing script.

"It's an older book, but I thought you might like it," Mark

told her. "I know how much you enjoyed *The Hobbit* and *Lord of the Rings*."

She ran her fingers over the beautiful book. "Thank you, Dad."

She handed him her wrapped package. "Merry Christmas."

He tore at the paper, ripping the neatly pressed edges and making Holly smile.

"*The Best of Calvin and Hobbes*," he read, smiling at the title. "Thank you, Holly."

They hugged and Holly tried not to think of how much she wished she could give Nathan his book now as well.

"Dad, there's something I need to tell you," she said after a moment. She chewed on her bottom lip and finally just took a sip of her rum for courage.

"You can tell me anything," Mark said. He held the book close to his chest, proud of his newest acquisition.

"Dad..." She closed her eyes. Better just to get this over with. "Nathan isn't keeping ECT here. He's back to moving it again."

"Oh."

The one sound held soft surprise, heartbreak, and acceptance all at once. Holly searched her father's face, worried about what she would see there. Defeat filled his features and he seemed to age ten years in the space of seconds.

"I'm so sorry, Dad," she told him. "I shouldn't have told you in the first place and gotten your hopes up."

"No, no I'm glad you did," Mark countered. "I got to spend the last day happy. I didn't worry about the party tomorrow as much because I thought we would have more." Mark shrugged. "Now, I don't have to worry."

Holly wished she could sink into the floor. Mark was taking this too well. The fact that tomorrow's party would be the last of the bookstore's Christmases made her want to cry. It was a staple for the town.

It was the end of an era that she'd never thought would happen.

Not to mention all her students. She thought of Jenifer, Molly and Jake. This would be their last Christmas in Colorado. The last one in their current home. She hoped for their sake that it was a good one.

"Where's that rum?" Mark asked, looking around. Holly handed him the small bottle on the floor next to her. Mark took a swig straight from the bottle. "Is that why Nathan isn't here tonight?"

Holly nodded. "We decided things weren't going to work out. And he had to work."

It sounded lame, but it was true.

"I'm so sorry, sweetheart." Mark reached out and squeezed her hand. "I thought he was the one, but..."

"Yeah, me too." Holly held out her hand for the rum and her dad handed it to her. She took a swig and then handed it back.

"Well, it could be worse," Mark said after a moment.

Holly lifted her brows. "How?"

He reached for the rum. "We could be out of rum. And at least there's chocolate chip cookies in the kitchen."

Holly chuckled, even though she felt like sobbing. She'd already cried today. She didn't want to cry. It was Christmas Eve, for heaven's sake. People were supposed to be happy, not heartbroken.

"You going to be okay?" Mark asked her, watching her with the concerned eyes of a parent.

"We both will," she told him. She hoped it wasn't a lie.

He patted her arm and they both turned and stared into the fire.

Worst Christmas Eve ever, Holly decided.
And she took another sip of rum.

CHAPTER 42

$\mathcal{H}$olly

HOLLY DIDN'T WANT to open her eyes. She had the covers pulled up around her chin and her body was comfortably warm, but her face was cold. If she opened her eyes, that meant it was morning.

And for the first time in her life, she didn't want it to be Christmas morning.

Her phone began to buzz, telling her that it was almost time to leave. She had to be at the store an hour before the party to get everything set up.

With a groan, she sat up, swung her feet out of bed, and immediately regretted the decision. Her apartment was freezing. Even with socks on, her feet were cold on the floor. She hurried to the bathroom, changing her clothes as quickly as possible before the cold could set in.

Luckily, she'd had enough water that she wasn't too hung over. Just a mild headache and she didn't want any breakfast.

240

She grabbed her things and paused at the small Christmas tree in her living room. Three presents sat under it. There was the big, bulky Christmas present for her father, a hand-made fleece blanket she'd put together for him, and the two presents for Nathan. Seeing them made her heart ache.

"Someone else might as well enjoy them," she said to herself, picking up all three and bringing them into the car with her. She was going to a Christmas party where gifts would be given to anyone and everyone. Surely, there was someone in town that would like a copy of *The Christmas Carol* and a large Devonsville T-shirt.

The ride to her father's bookstore was cold. She tried to enjoy the fresh snow on the trees, the white and blue of the mountains, and the twinkle of lights in every pine tree, but she felt hollow inside.

She missed Nathan. She wondered what he was doing this Christmas morning. Probably working, she decided. She told herself not to cry, but she couldn't help it.

She had to pull over to the side of the road and let the tears come. She cried until she couldn't breathe. Luckily, there was almost no traffic since it was Christmas morning, so no one saw her. When she finally felt in control again, she wiped her face, checked her mascara in the rear-view mirror, and continued on to the bookstore.

She went in through the back, following the sound of Christmas music to the front room. Mark was already setting up. He wore jeans and a red sweater with a Christmas tree proudly sewn into the front.

"Merry Christmas, sweetheart," he greeted Holly as soon as he saw her. He came over, wrapping her up in a hug and a kiss on the head.

"Hi, Dad," she said, snuggling her face into the safety of his embrace. For a moment, she let herself be a child again. "Merry Christmas."

He held onto her until she let go. He knew she was struggling with Nathan's leaving.

"Thanks," she said, wiping her cheeks and pulling away from her father. "We should get things set up."

Mark nodded. "I'll set up the tables for food. You finish the wrapping on the gifts. I don't think there's much left."

Holly left her father pulling on tables and straightening tablecloths to go up to his office. He had most of the gifts in a big red velvet bag. This year, there was only the one bag. She could remember earlier years where there had been up to five red velvet bags, all stuffed to the brim with stuffed animals, books, and toys.

This year, there were just some books. They were thin and cheap. The toys were plastic things from China that they'd ordered in bulk. It was a meager offering for the store, but it was all they had to offer. With Elements leaving, the store didn't have enough customers to afford more.

It would have to be enough. Holly hoped the kids wouldn't be disappointed. She always made sure that the low-income kids got something extra, but this year she was scraping by. She'd put most of her extra money into the cheap plastic things from China, just so that there would be more in the bag.

Holly wrapped the last few books and carefully tucked them into the bag. The Santa suit hung in the small closet to the side of the desk. Mark made sure it was immaculate and she ran her fingers across the soft satin.

She could remember as a girl the magic of Santa. As an adult, she knew the secret and while she enjoyed being the gift-giver, some days she missed the magic of being a child. This year especially.

With a sigh, she went back down and helped her father with the last minute decorations.

Finally, everything was ready. She turned on the lights for

the big tree at the front of the bookstore and opened the door. Already there was a line of people waiting for the annual Christmas party.

A stream of people came into the store, everyone carrying delicious smelling food to the tables. Kids ran around telling one another what magical things Santa brought them while the parents sipped on coffee and shared their midnight bike-instruction putting-together woes.

The atmosphere was happy, but subdued. Everyone knew this was the last one of these and they were trying to enjoy it without becoming sad. It was a fine line. Holly was certainly struggling with it.

"Okay, Dad," Holly whispered to her father a little past noon. The food was mostly eaten and the kids were growing restless. "I think it's time for Santa to arrive."

Mark winked and excused himself. He headed upstairs to change into his Santa costume and in a few minutes he would come around the front with his bag of toys to surprise the children. Holly went to the far end of the room and began cleaning up the food.

"Great party," Aliyah said, coming up alongside Holly. She helped stack empty plates and pick up utensils. "Did you try the cinnamon rolls? They were amazing."

"I know, right? Mrs. Gonzalez said she'd give me the recipe. I think I might have a new teacher potluck dish," Holly replied.

"You doing okay?" Aliyah asked, watching her friend's face. "Do you need me to get you ice cream? Brownies?"

"I'm okay," Holly promised. "Or, I will be. Maybe we can eat ice cream tomorrow and complain about men. I could use a day of that."

"Done," Aliyah promised. She gave her friend a hug. "You let me know. I'm here for you."

"Thanks," Holly said, forcing a smile.

"Wow. Your dad was fast," Aliyah said, pointing to the front door. "I thought he just went upstairs. Usually it takes him forever to change."

Holly frowned. Usually it did take her dad a long time to get into costume. He always took extra care attaching the beard for this so that the kids could tug on it and not have the secret ruined. The glue took a long time to dry.

Yet, there was Santa at the front door.

"Ho, ho, ho! Merry Christmas!" boomed Santa, throwing open the front door to the bookstore. The kids all cheered and ran to gather around the jolly old man.

That's when Holly noticed that Santa didn't have the right red velvet bag. Instead, he had several dark red bags. Six of them. He settled himself in the large comfortable chair by the Christmas tree, ready to give out his gifts.

"Where's Jake?" Santa asked, pulling out a present from one of the bags.

"Here!" Jake called, coming in from the back. Jake was one of Holly's students and had a deep love of dogs. Unfortunately, he was also very allergic.

"This is for you," Santa told him, handing him a beautiful stuffed dog toy. As soon as it was in Jake's hands, it became alive, barking and wagging its tail.

"It's a robot dog!" Jake shouted, joy turning his surprise into joy. "Thank you, Santa!"

Holly stopped putting things away and began walking toward this strange Santa.

"Where's Molly?" Santa asked, looking around.

"Here," said the small girl, coming up to him shyly.

"Merry Christmas, Molly," Santa told her, handing her something from the bag. It was a big, fluffy unicorn.

Molly loved unicorns. She shrieked with delight.

These were not the toys Mark and Holly had bought for the kids. And that was not her father in the Santa costume.

Who was this impostor Santa? Holly frowned, making her way slowly toward him. She didn't want to startle the kids. The last thing she wanted was to make a scene and ruin the image of Santa for them.

"Where's Marcos?" Santa asked, reaching into a bag. He pulled out a bright shiny red sled, handing it to her bright-eyed student.

"Where's Anna?" Santa asked, looking around. Again, another one of Holly's students.

"Here, Santa," said the small girl, looking up hopefully. He handed her a giant bin of Legos and the poor girl looked like she was about to pass out.

"Oh, Santa," she cried. "How did you know? This is *exactly* what I wanted!"

Anna threw her arms around Santa's neck and kissed his cheek before picking up her Legos and running to her mother with the world's biggest smile on her face.

A dog? A unicorn, a sled, Legos... somehow all these toys sounded familiar. Holly tried to place how she knew what each of her students wanted and then remembered the snowflakes from her classroom.

"Where's Ms. Jones?" Santa asked, looking around the room. Holly startled, unsure of what to do now that she was called out.

"She's there!" Molly shouted, and soon she had three kids dragging her across the room and toward Santa.

The closer she got, the more she knew for certain that this was not her father. Especially when she looked toward the back and saw her father leaning against the door to his office. He wasn't wearing the Santa suit.

"Come sit on Santa's lap and tell me what you want for Christmas," Santa said, motioning to Holly. She frowned. She knew that voice. Her eyes went wide.

Nathan.

She looked up and into Santa's brown eyes. Only, they were Nathan's brown eyes.

Holly's heart stopped in her chest. The only reason she continued to move was the fact that her students were dragging her across the floor to see Santa. The kids pushed her into the open space in front of Santa and waited to see what happened next.

"You have to sit on his lap, Ms. Jones," Jake informed her. "You have to do what Santa says."

"Oh. Right." Holly sat on Santa's knee, more because she was going to pass out if she kept standing than because she was supposed to.

She stared wide-eyed in wonder at the man before her. Nathan wore a red Santa suit with a beautiful white snowy beard. His eyes were dark and just for her. The whole room seemed to fade away as he looked at her.

"And what do you want for Christmas, Ms. Jones?" Nathan's voice was soft.

"I'm not sure," she managed to say. "I'm not sure if Santa can bring me what I want."

"I'm here," he whispered, just loud enough for Holly to hear.

She swallowed hard. "Really?"

"I'm here to stay, Holly. I'm not leaving you again."

She leaned forward, wanting to kiss him but he stopped her.

"Not in front of the kids." He motioned with his head towards the very interested group of children and adults watching them.

Holly's cheeks flamed red. She'd forgotten they were even there.

"I need to discuss something with Ms. Jones," Santa said, raising his voice. "But, since I have so many more gifts to give out, I'm going to have my elves help me."

He motioned and two men stepped forward.

Holly recognized them as Hal and Gregory, Nathan's bodyguards. However, they were wearing green tunics with striped red tights and a yellow belt. They also had on elf ears and pointed caps. They looked more like a pair of Jolly Green Giants than Santa's helpers.

Hal went to the open bag. "Where is Natasha?"

Natasha stepped forward, fear and curiosity on her face. "That's me."

"Here you go, darling," Hal said, a smile filling his face as he handed her an art kit.

Natasha beamed and threw her arms around him, giving him a huge hug. Hal looked like this was the happiest day of his life.

"I don't think I've ever seen him smile," Nathan remarked, standing up and taking Holly's hand. He pulled her toward the back and Mark opened the door up to his office. While the kids were busy watching the two giant elves pull out presents, Holly and Santa slipped upstairs.

CHAPTER 43

*N*athan

THE WALK up the small flight of stairs to Mark's office was the longest one of Nathan's life. He could feel Holly's hand in his, but he still had to keep looking back and making sure she was real.

They stepped into the office, and Holly closed the door behind her.

"Are you really here?" she asked, a hint of fear in her voice and eyes. "I thought you said you didn't think this was going to work."

"It wasn't the way things were," he told her. "But, I made changes. I hope I haven't missed my chance."

"No." She shook her head and smiled. "You haven't missed it. But I need to know you aren't going to leave again. That we're not just going to end up in the same place as before."

Nathan reached into the back pocket of his Santa

costume and pulled out a piece of heavy paper. He handed it to her.

"This says you're the owner of Elements Computer Technologies," Holly said, reading the paper. She looked up at him still confused. "I thought you were always the owner."

"No. Paradigm was the owner," he explained. "I bought it from them."

It took her a moment to process what he just told her. Her eyes went wide and her mouth dropped open.

"I bought Elements Computer Technologies from Paradigm," he explained. "They aren't moving to California anymore because I don't want them to. I want the company to stay here where it belongs. They are staying in Devonsville."

"What about Paradigm?" Holly asked, staring down at the paper. "What about you?"

"I quit."

"What?"

Nathan wasn't sure her eyes could get much bigger or that her jaw could go much lower. He took her hands in his, setting the paper on Mark's desk behind him.

"I quit. I'm not the CEO for Paradigm anymore," he told her. "I own ECT and that's my only business now. Even with that, I'm not going to be the CEO. I just want to build things again."

He'd gone to the board meeting and told them he wanted to buy ECT. The board had been shocked. They were stunned when he told them he was quitting as well.

Fauna had been right. They were happy to have a reason to let him go. The lawyers had been called in for an emergency settlement, but Nathan had walked out with ownership of Elements. It hadn't even cost him as much as he thought it would.

Paradigm was no longer where he wanted to be. It wasn't

who he was anymore. The money wasn't what made him want to get up in the morning. He was still a billionaire. He didn't need more money than that.

He'd told the board to promote Lucy. He hoped she'd find her way to the top of the company. She wouldn't be pleased with the sale of ECT, but she would survive. She would make money because that was what mattered to her.

It didn't matter to him like it used to.

Holly mattered.

For him, he couldn't wait to just be an owner. Someone else could be the CEO. He planned on keeping the company mostly the way it was now, just focusing even more on innovation. He wanted to be one of the innovators again.

"Nathan…"

"I want to create things again," he told her. "I don't want to manage things. No more meetings. No more board meetings to discuss how the stock market will respond to market changes. I don't want that life anymore."

"So, you'll be here?" The hope in her voice made his heart quiver.

"If you'll have me," he told her.

"Yes," she whispered. "Yes, I'll have you."

And she kissed him, beard and all.

"The beard is terrible," she told him, pulling back with a laugh. He tugged it off to the side, revealing his face to her. She touched his cheek, her eyes full of happy tears. "You're really here?"

"I'm really here," he promised. "You are what matter. You, me, us – we're everything."

She kissed him again, tears streaming down her face. He held her to him, crying and laughing himself. This was all he could have ever wanted for Christmas. Christmas was now his favorite holiday.

"So you're my Christmas present," Holly said, her eyes smiling with joy.

"If you'll have me."

"You're just what I asked Santa for," she told him.

"Red suit and all?" he asked, nuzzling her cheek.

She laughed. "Red suit and all."

And he kissed her.

DOWNSTAIRS, Jake came running from the stairs with Mark glaring at him. Mark shooed him away from the back room and chased him toward where the elves were still handing out toys, having the time of their lives.

"Guys, guys!" Jake told his friends. "You're never going to believe this, but I saw Ms. Jones kissing Santa Claus!"

CHAPTER 44

$\mathcal{M}$erryweather

"WELL, THAT WORKED OUT MARVELOUSLY," Merryweather said to Flora.

"I agree. I was a little worried there for a bit," Flora told her. "But Fauna did a marvelous job."

"Fauna did a marvelous job?" Merryweather asked, raising an eyebrow.

"And you," Flora said, obviously appeasing her. "What will happen next for them?"

"A happily ever after," Merryweather replied. "A happily ever after."

"That is the best kind of magic," Flora said with a smile. "A happily ever after with Christmas. It doesn't get better than that."

Merryweather had to agree.

An American Cinderella: A Royal Love Story

*"I'D GIVE **up my whole kingdom to be with you. I want to be your Prince Charming.**"*

ARIA HAS a big heart but bigger problems. Her whole life is a mess thanks to her controlling stepmother. But when she's knocked over- literally- by the hottest man she's ever had the pleasure of tangling up her body with, everything changes.

Henry Prescott, second-string rugby player for the Paradisa Royals, is funny, sweet, charming, and oh-so-sexy. He's got a rock hard body and tackles her in bed as fiercely as he tackled her in the park. Knowing nothing about rugby, but absolutely intoxicated by his accent, she finds herself falling for him.

There's only one problem: Henry Prescott doesn't exist.

The man she thinks she loves is actually Prince Henry,

second in line for the throne of the nation of Paradisa. He's the man who Aria's entire department has to impress for trade relations. And that makes Aria's stepmother's plans even more dangerous.

He's the man who could destroy her world or make all her dreams come true.

He lied about being a prince... did he also lie about being in love?

NYT Bestseller Krista Lakes brings you this brand new sweet-and-sexy royal romance. This standalone novel will have you cheering for an American princess's happily ever after.

An American Cinderella: A Royal Love Story

Further reading:

Bad Boys and Babies
    Family Doctor's Baby
    The Billionaire's Baby Arrangement
    Crime Boss Baby

Kinds of Love
    A Forever Kind of Love
    A Wonderful Kind of Love

An Endless Kind of Love

Billionaires and Brides
    Yours Completely: A Cinderella Love Story
    Yours Truly: A Cinderella Love Story
    Yours Royally: A Cinderella Love Story

The "Kisses" series
    Saltwater Kisses: A Billionaire Love Story
    Kisses From Jack: The Other Side of Saltwater Kisses
    Rainwater Kisses: A Billionaire Love Story
    Champagne Kisses: A Timeless Love Story
    Freshwater Kisses: A Billionaire Love Story
    Sandcastle Kisses: A Billionaire Love Story
    Hurricane Kisses: A Billionaire Love Story
    Barefoot Kisses: A Billionaire Love Story
    Sunrise Kisses: A Billionaire Love Story
    Waterfall Kisses: A Billionaire Love Story
    Island Kisses: A Billionaire Love Story

Other Novels
    I Choose You: A Secret Billionaire Romance
    His Every Desire: A Billionaire Seduction
    Wolf Six's Salvation: A Shifter Love Story
    Burned: A New Adult Love Story
    Walking on Sunshine: A Sweet Summer Romance
    An American Cinderella: A Royal Love Story
    Mr. Darcy's Kiss: A Contemporary Pride and Prejudice